Before I Fall

JESSICA SCOTT

Printed in the United States of America

First Printing 2015

ISBN: 978-1-942102-16-8

Author photo courtesy of Buzz Covington Photography
Cover design by Jessica Scott
For more information please see www.jessicascott.net

DEDICATION

To my real life stats savior
You know who you are

ALSO BY JESSICA SCOTT

Falling Series

Before I Fall
Break My Fall (Forthcoming)

The Homefront Series

Homefront
After the War
Face the Fire

The Coming Home Series

Because of You (ebook)
I'll Be Home for Christmas: A Coming Home Novella (ebook)
Anything for You: A Coming Home Short Story
Back to You
Until There Was You (ebook)
All For You
It's Always Been You
All I Want for Christmas is You: A Coming Home Novella

Nonficton

To Iraq & Back: On War and Writing
The Long Way Home: One Mom's Journey Home from War

Before I Fall

Chapter One

Beth

My dad has good days and bad. The good days are awesome. When he's awake and he's pretending to cook and I'm pretending to eat it. It's a joke between us that he burns water. But that's okay.

On the good days, I humor him. Because for those brief interludes, I have my dad back.

The not so good days, like today, are more common. Days when he can't get out of bed without my help.

I bring him his medication. I know exactly how much he takes and how often.

And I know exactly when he runs out.

I've gotten better at keeping up with his appointments so he doesn't, but the faceless bastards at the VA cancel more than they keep. But what can we do? He can't get private insurance with his health, and because someone decided that his back injury wasn't entirely service-related, he doesn't have a high enough disability rating to qualify for automatic care. So we wait for them to fit him in and when we can't, we go to the emergency room and the bills pile up. Because despite him not being able to move on the bad days, his back pain treatments are elective.

So I juggle phone calls to the docs and try to keep us above water.

Bastards.

I leave his phone by his bed and make sure it's plugged in to charge before I head to school. He's got water and the pills he'll need when he finally comes out of the fog. Our tiny house is only a mile from campus. Not in the best part of town but not the worst either. I've got an hour before class, which means I need to hustle. Thankfully, it's not terribly hot today so I won't arrive on campus a sweating, soggy mess. That always makes a good impression, especially at a wealthy southern school like this one.

I make it to campus with twenty minutes to spare and check my e-mail on the campus WiFi. I can't check it at the house - Internet is a luxury we can't afford. If I'm lucky, my neighbor's signal sometimes bleeds over into our house. Most of the time, though, I'm not that lucky. Which is fine. Except for days like this where there's a note from my professor asking me to come by her office before class.

Professor Blake is terrifying to those who don't know her. She's so damn smart it's scary, and she doesn't let any of us get away with not speaking up in class. Sit up straight. Speak loudly. She's harder on the girls, too. Some of the underclassmen complain that she's being unfair. I don't complain, though. I know she's doing it for a reason.

"You got my note just in time," she says. Her tortoise-shell glasses reflect the fluorescent light, and I can't see her eyes.

"Yes, ma'am." She's told me not to call her ma'am, but it slips out anyway. I can't help it. Thankfully, she doesn't push the issue.

"I have a job for you."

"Sure." A job means extra money on the side. Money that I can use to get my dad his medications. Or, you know, buy food. Little things. It's hard as hell to do stats when your stomach is rumbling. "What does it entail?"

"Tutoring. Business statistics."

"I hear a but in there."

"He's a former soldier."

Once, when my mom first left us, I couldn't wake my dad

up. My blood pounded so loud in my ears that I could hardly hear. That's how I feel now. My mouth is open, but no sound crosses my lips. Professor Blake knows how I feel about the war, about soldiers. I can't deal with all the hoah chest-beating bullshit. Not with my dad and everything the war has done to him.

"Before you say no, hear me out. Noah has some very well-placed friends that want him very much to succeed here. He's got a ticket into the business school graduate program, but only if he gets through Stats."

I'm having a hard time breathing. I can't do this. Just thinking about what the war has done to my dad makes it difficult to breathe. But the idea of extra money, just a little, is a strong motivator when you don't have it. Principles are for people who can afford them.

I take a deep, cleansing breath. "So why me?"

"Because you've got the best head for stats I've seen in a long time, and I've seen you explain things to the underclassmen in ways that make sense to them. You can translate."

"There's no one else?" I hate that I need this job.

Professor Blake removes her glasses with a quiet sigh. "Our school is very pro-military, Beth. And I would consider it a personal favor if you'd help him."

She's right. That's the only reason I was able to get in. This is one of the Southern Ivies. A top school in the southeast that I have no business being at except for my dad, who knew the dean of the law school from his time in the army. I hate the war and everything it's done to my family. But I wouldn't be where I am today if my dad hadn't gone to war and sacrificed everything to make sure I had a future outside of our crappy little place outside of Fort Benning. There are things worse than death and my dad lives with them every day because he had done what he had to do to provide for me.

I will not let him down.

"Okay. When do I start?"

She hands me a slip of paper. It's yellow and has her

letterhead at the top in neat, formal block letters. "Here's his information. Make contact and see what his schedule is." She places her glasses back on and just like that, I'm dismissed.

Professor Blake is not a warm woman, but I wouldn't have made it through my first semester at this school without her mentorship. If not for her and my friend Abby, I would have left from the sheer overwhelming force of being surrounded by money and wealth and all the intangibles that came along with it. I did not belong here, but because of Professor Blake, I hadn't quit.

So if I need to tutor some blockhead soldier to repay her kindness, then so be it. Graduating from this program is my one chance to take care of my dad and I will not fail.

Noah

I hate being on campus. I feel old. Which isn't entirely logical because I'm only a few years older than most of the kids plugged in and tuned out around me. Part of me envies them. The casual nonchalance as they stroll from class to class, listening to music without a care in the world.

It feels surreal. Like a dream that I'm going to wake up from any minute now and find that I'm still in Iraq with LT and the guys. A few months ago, I was patrolling a shithole town in the middle of Iraq where we had no official boots on the ground and now I'm here. I feel like I've been ripped out of my normal.

Hell, I don't even know what to wear to class. This is not a problem I've had for the last few years.

I erred on the side of caution - khakis and a button-down polo. I hope I don't look like a fucking douchebag. LT would be proud of me. I think. But he's not here to tell me what to do, and I'm so far out of my fucking league it's not even funny.

I almost grin at the thought. LT is still looking after me. His parents are both academics, and it is because of him that I am even here. I told him there was no fucking way I was going to make it into the business school because math was basically a foreign language to me. He said tough shit and had helped me apply.

My phone vibrates in my pocket, distracting me from the fact that my happy ass is lost on campus. Kind of hard to navigate when the terrain is buildings and mopeds as opposed to burned-out city streets and destroyed mosques.

Stats tutor contact info: Beth Lamont. E-mail her, don't text.

Apparently, LT was serious about making sure I didn't fail. Class hasn't even started yet, and here I am with my very own tutor. I'm paying for it out of pocket. There were limits to how much pride I could swallow.

Half the students around me looked like they'd turn sixteen shades of purple if I said the wrong thing. Like, look out, here's the crazy-ass veteran, one bad day away from shooting the place up. The other half probably expects the former soldier to speak in broken English and be barely literate because we're too poor and dumb to go to college. Douchebags. It's bad enough that I wanted to put on my ruck and get the hell out of this place.

I stop myself. I need to get working on that whole cussing thing, too. Can't be swearing like I'm back with the guys or calling my classmates names. Not if I wanted to fit in and not be the angry veteran stereotype.

I'm not sure about this. Not any of it. I never figured I was the college type - at least not this kind of college.

I tap out an e-mail to the tutor and ask when she's available to meet. The response comes back quickly. A surprise, really. I can't tell you how many e-mails I sent trying to get my schedule fixed and nothing. Silence. Hell, the idea of actually responding to someone seems foreign. I had to physically go to the registrar's office to get a simple question answered about a form. No one would answer a damn e-mail, and you could forget about a phone call. Sometimes, I think they'd be more comfortable with carrier pigeons. Or not having to interact at all. I can't imagine what my old platoon would do to this place.

Noon at The Grind.

Which is about as useful information as giving me

directions in Arabic because I have no idea a) what The Grind is or b) where it might be.

I respond to her e-mail and tell her that, saving her contact information in my phone. If she's going to be my tutor, who knows when I'll need to get a hold of her in a complete panic.

Library coffee shop. Central campus.

Okay then. This ought to be interesting.

I head to my first class. Business Statistics. Great. Guess I'll get my head wrapped around it before I meet the tutor. That should be fun.

I'm pretty sure that fun and statistics don't belong in the same sentence but whatever. It's a required course, so I guess that's where I'm going to be.

My hands start sweating the minute I step into the classroom. Hello, school anxiety. Fuck. I forgot how much I hate school. I snag a seat at the back of the room, the wall behind me so I can see the doors and windows. I hate the idea of someone coming in behind me. Call it PTSD or whatever, but I hate not being able to see who's coming or going.

I reach into my backpack and pull out a small pill bottle. My anxiety is tripping at a double-time, and I'm going to have a goddamned heart attack at this rate.

I hate the pills more than I hate being in a classroom again, but there's not much I can do about it. Not if I want to do this right.

And LT would pretty much haunt me if I fuck this up.

I choke down the bitter pill and pull out my notebook as the rest of the class filters in.

I flip to the back of the notebook and start taking notes. Observations. Old habit from Iraq. Keeps me sane, I guess.

The females have some kind of religious objection to pants. Yoga pants might as well be full-on burqas. I've seen actual tights being worn as outer garments and no one bats an eye. It feels strange seeing so much flesh after being in Iraq where the only flesh you saw was burned and bloody...

Well, wasn't *that* a happy fucking thought.

Jesus. I scrub my hands over my face. Need to put that shit

aside, a.s.a.p.

Professor Blake comes in, and I immediately turn my attention to the front of the classroom. She looks stern today, but that's a front. She's got to look mean in front of these young kids. She's nothing like she was when we talked about enrollment before I started. She was one of the few people who did respond to e-mails at this place.

"Good morning. I'm Professor Blake, and this is my TA Beth Lamont. If you have problems or issues, go to her. She speaks for me and has my full faith and confidence. If you want to pass this class, pay attention because she knows this information inside and out."

Beth Lamont. *Hello, tutor.*

I lose the rest of whatever Professor Blake has to say. Because Beth Lamont is like some kind of stats goddess. Add in that she's drop-dead smoking hot, but it's her eyes that grab hold of me. Piercing green, so bright that you can see them from across the room. She looks at me, and I can feel my entire body standing at the position of attention. It's been a long time since a woman made me stand up and take notice. And I'm supposed to focus on stats around her? I'll be lucky to remember how to write my name in crayons around her.

I am completely fucked.

Chapter Two

Beth

It doesn't take me long to figure out who Noah Warren is. He's a little bit older than the rest of the fresh-faced underclassmen I've gotten used to. I'm not even twenty-one, but I feel ancient these days. I was up late last night, worrying about my dad.

I can feel him watching me as I hand out the syllabus and the first lecture notes. My hackles are up - he's staring and being rude. I don't tolerate this from the jocks but right then, I'm stuck because Professor Blake has asked me to tutor him. I can't exactly cuss him out in front of the class.

Which is really frustrating because the rest of the class is focused on Professor Blake, but not our soldier. Oh no, he's such a stereotype it's not even funny. Staring. Not even trying to be slick about it like the football player in the front of the classroom who's trying to catch a glimpse of my tits when I lean down to pass out the papers.

Instead, our soldier just leans back, nonchalant like he owns the place. Like the whole world should bend over and kiss his ass because he's defending our freedom. Well, I know all about that, and the price is too goddamned high.

And wow, how is that for bitterness and angst on a

Monday morning? I need to get my shit together. I haven't even spoken to him and I'm already tarring and feathering him. Not going to be very productive for our tutoring relationship if I hate him before we even get started.

I take a deep breath and hand him the syllabus and the first lecture worksheet.

I imagine he's figured out that I'm his tutor.

I turn back and head to my desk in the front as Professor Blake drops her bombshell on the class.

"There will be no computer use in this class. You may use laptops during lab when Beth is instructing because there will be practical applications. But during lecture, you will not use computers. If your phones go off, you can expect to be docked participation points, and those are a significant portion of your grade."

There is the requisite crying and wailing and gnashing of the teeth. I remember the first time I heard of Professor Blake's no computer rule. I thought it was draconian and complete bullshit. But then I realized she was right - I learned better by writing things down. Especially the stats stuff.

I look up at Noah. He's watching the class now. He's scowling. He looks like he might frown a lot. He looks...harder than the rest of the class. There are angles to his cheeks and shadows beneath his eyes. His dark hair is shorter than most and he damn sure doesn't have that crazy-ass swoop thing that so many of the guys are doing these days.

Everything about him radiates soldier. I wonder if he knows how intimidating he looks. And why the hell do I care what he thinks?

I'm going to be his tutor, not his shrink.

He shifts and his gaze collides with mine. Something tightens in the vicinity of my belly. It's not fear. Soldiers don't scare me, not even ones who look like they were forged in fire like Noah.

No, it's something else. Something tight and tense and distinctly distracting. I'm not in the mood for my hormones to overwhelm my common sense.

I stomp on the feeling viciously.

I'm staring at him now. I'm deliberately trying to look confident and confrontational. Men like Noah don't respect weakness. Show a moment's hesitation and the next thing you know they've got your ass pinned in a corner while they're trying to grab your tits.

He lifts one brow in response. I have no idea how to read that reaction.

Noah

I had to swallow my pride and ask some perky blond directions to The Grind. I hadn't expected Valley Girl airheadedness but then again, I didn't really know what I expected. I managed to interpret the directions between a few giggles and several "likes" and "ahs" and "ums". I imagined her briefing my CO and almost smiled at the train wreck it would be. We had a lieutenant like her once. She was in the intelligence shop and she might have been the smartest lieutenant in the brigade, but the way she talked made everyone think she was a complete space cadet.

She'd said "like" one too many times during a briefing to the division commander and yeah, well, last I heard, she'd been put in charge of keeping the latrines cleaned down in Kuwait. Which wasn't fair but then again, what in life was? Guess the meat eaters in the brigade hadn't wanted to listen to the Valley Girl give them intelligence reports on what the Kurdish Pesh and ISIS were up to at any given point in time.

My cup of coffee from The Grind isn't terrible. It certainly isn't Green Bean coffee, but it's a passable second place. Green Bean has enough caffeine in it to keep you up for two days straight. This stuff...it's softer, I guess. Smoother? I'm not really sure. It isn't bad. Just not what I'm used to. Nothing here is.

I wonder if there is any way to run down to Bragg and get some of the hard stuff. Hell, I am considering chewing on coffee beans at this point. Anything to clear the fog in my brain.

But I need the fog to keep the anxiety at bay, so I guess I'm fucked there, too. Guess I should start getting used to things around here. No better place to start than with the coffee, I guess.

The Grind is busy. Small, low tables are crowded with laptops and books and students all looking intently at their work. It's like a morgue in here. Everyone is hyper-focused. Don't these people know how to have a good time? Relax a little bit? There are no seats anywhere. The Grind is apparently a popular if silent, place.

The tutor walks in at exactly twelve fifty-eight. Two minutes to spare.

"You're not late." I'm mildly shocked.

She does that eyebrow thing again, and I have to admit on her, it is pretty fucking sexy. "I tend to be punctual. It's a life skill."

"Kitty has claws," I say.

She stiffens. Apparently, the joke's fallen flat. Guess I'm going to have to work on that.

"Let's get something straight, shall we? My name is Beth, and I'm going to tutor you in business stats. We are not going to be friends or fuck buddies or anything else you might think of. I'm not 'Kitty' or any other pet name. I'm here to get a degree, not a husband."

My not-strong-enough coffee burns my tongue as her words sink in. She's damn sure prickly all right. I can't decide if I admire her spine or I think it's unnecessary. Hell, it isn't like I tried to grab her ass or asked her to suck my dick.

The coffee slides down my throat. "Glad we cleared that up," I say instead. "I wasn't sure if blowjobs came with the tutoring."

She grinds her teeth. There isn't much by way of sense of humor in the tutor. She has a no-nonsense look about her. Her dark blond hair is drawn tight to her neck, and I can't figure out if she is naturally flawless or if she is just damn good with makeup.

There is a freshness to her, though, that isn't something I

am used to either. Enlisted women, the few I've been around, either try way too hard with too much black eyeliner downrange or aren't interested in men beyond the buddy level.

But this academic woman is a new species entirely for me, and as our standoff continues, I realize I have no idea what the rules of engagement are with someone like her. At least not beyond her name is not Kitty and she's not here for a husband. Oh and can't forget the no blowjobs thing. She made the rules pretty clear.

She is fucking stunning and I suddenly can't talk.

She clears her throat. "So are we going to stand here and continue to stare at each other, or are we going to get to work? I have somewhere to be in two hours."

I motion toward the library. "Lead the way."

Beth

He's watching my ass as I walk in front of him. He's just the type who would do something like that. The blowjob comment caught me completely off guard. I hate that. I hate that I couldn't come up with any brilliant, sarcastic response, either. I always think of smartass comebacks fifteen minutes too late.

So now I am even more irritated than I was when he'd been staring at me class. What the hell had Professor Blake been thinking?

I lead us to a small table out of the way, where there won't be a lot of disruption. Stats is one of those things that takes a lot of concentration. At least it did for me until I learned the language.

I pull out the worksheet from class. Homework and lessons. "So let's get the business stuff out of the way," I say. I hate the tone in my voice. I'm not normally a ball-busting bitch, but he's set me off and if being cold and curt is the only way to keep him in line then so be it. "I'd like to be paid each meeting. Cash."

"What's your rate?"

I sit back. How the hell did that question catch me off guard? I don't know. I work part-time at the country club next to campus, but the tips are hit or miss. The thing about the wealthy? Some of them can be downright stingy. Most of the time, I make okay tips. When it isn't, I tried not to be bitter about how they don't need the money like I do.

I just smile and take their orders.

I'm stuck. Noah is not my first tutoring job, but my other jobs were paid for by the university. I have no idea how much to charge for freelance work.

"Fifty dollars an hour, three times a week," he offers abruptly.

I cover my shock with my hand. "Huh?"

"Fifty dollars an hour. I saw a sign in the common area charging that much for Spanish. Figure Stats should be at least that much, right?"

My voice is stuck somewhere in the bottom of my chest. Fifty bucks an hour is a lot of groceries and medication. It feels wrong taking that kind of money, even from Mr. Does-the-Tutoring-Come-with-Blowjobs.

"Will that be a problem?"

I shake my head. "No. That's fine." There's a stack of bills that need to be paid. The electricity is a week overdue. I'm counting on tips tonight to make a payment tomorrow to keep them from shutting it off. Again. Between that and the money from tutoring - I could keep the lights on. I can feel my face burning hot. I turn away, digging into my backpack to keep him from seeing my humiliation, not wanting him to see my relief.

"Same time, same place? Monday, Wednesday and Friday?" My computer flickers to life.

"Works for me. How much pain should I be prepared for?" He sounds worried. He should. Professor Blake is one of the top in her field, and that's no small feat considering she came up at a time when women were still blazing trails in the business world.

"Depends on if you do the work or not," I say. I can't

quite bring myself to offer him comfort. I'm still irritated by the blowjob comment. "So let's get started." I lean over the worksheet. "What questions do you have from class today?"

I look up to find him watching me. There's something in his eyes that tugs at me. I don't want to be tugged at.

He looks away. He's strangling that poor pen in his hands. Clearly, I've struck a nerve with my question.

I wish I didn't remember how that felt. The lost sensation of not having a clue what I was doing. I didn't even know what questions to ask.

I don't want to feel anything charitable toward him, but there's something about the way he shifts. Something that makes him vulnerable.

I run my tongue over my teeth. This isn't going well. "Okay look. We'll start with the basics, okay?"

I open my laptop to the lecture notes.

He finally notices my computer. "I haven't seen one of the black MacBooks in years," he says.

He's not being a prick, but I bristle anyway. "It might be old but she's never failed me."

"It can run stats software? Isn't that pretty intense processor-wise?"

I don't feel like telling him that to run said stats program, I have to shut down every other program and clear the cache. I don't want to admit that there's just no money to buy a new computer. I can't even finance one because I don't have the credit for it.

Business school is about looking the part as much as it is about knowing the game, so none of those words are going to leave my lips.

"It gets the job done," I say. "Now, the first lecture."

"I get everything about what stats is supposed to do. I got lost somewhere around regression."

"Don't worry about regression right now. We're going to focus on understanding what we're looking at first up. Basic concepts."

I look over at him. He's scowling at the paper. I can see

tiny flecks of gold in his dark brown eyes. He drags one hand through his short dark hair and leans forward. He's practically radiating tension, and I can feel it infecting me.

Damn it, I don't give a shit about his anxiety. I don't care. I can't.

"So the normal distribution is?"

I take a deep breath. This stuff I know. I draw the standard bell-shaped curve on his paper. "The normal distribution says that any results are normally..."

Noah

She knows her stuff. She relaxes when she starts talking about confidence intervals and normal distributions. Hell, I can't even *spell* normal distribution.

But she has a way of making things make sense.

And her confidence isn't scary so much as it is really fucking attractive.

I'm watching her lips move and I swear to God I'm trying to pay attention, but my brain decides to take a detour into not stats-ville. She's got a great mouth. It's a little too wide, and she has a tendency to chew on the inside of her lip when she's focusing.

I look down because I don't want her to catch me not paying attention. I need to understand this stuff, not stare at her like a lovesick private.

I'm focusing on confidence intervals when something dings on her computer. She frowns and opens her e-mail. It's angled away so I can't look over her shoulder, but something is clearly wrong. A flush creeps up her neck. She grinds her teeth when she's irritated. I tend to notice that in other people. I do the same thing when the anxiety starts taking hold. At least when it starts. It graduates quickly beyond teeth grinding into something more paralyzing.

I glance at my watch. It's almost time for her to go. I have no idea how I'm going to get my homework done, but I'll figure it out later. I'm meeting a couple of former military guys some place called Baywater Inn in a few hours. Plenty of time for me to get my homework done. Or at least attempt it. Because, of course, LT put me in touch with these guys, too.

But watching her, something is clearly wrong. I want to ask, but given how our history isn't exactly on the confide-your-darkest-secrets level, I don't.

She snaps her laptop closed and sighs. "I've got to run and make a phone call. Are you set for your assignment for lab?"

"I'll figure it out."

Her lips press into a flat line. "You can always look it up online."

"Sure thing."

She's distracted now. Not paying attention. I watch her move. There's an edge to her seriousness now, a tension in the long lines of her neck. A strand of hair falls free from the knot and brushes her temple. I want to tuck it back into place, but I'm pretty sure if I tried it, I'd be rewarded with a knee in the balls. And I like them where they are, thanks. I've come too close to losing them to risk them now.

I pull out my wallet and hand her two twenties and a ten. She hesitates then offers the ten back. "We didn't do the full hour." I refuse the money. "Keep it. Obviously you've got something to take care of. Don't worry about it."

She sucks in a deep breath like she's going to argue but then clamps her mouth shut. "Thank you."

She didn't choke on it, but it's a close thing. I am suddenly deeply curious about what has gotten her all wound up in such a short amount of time.

Maybe I'll get a chance to ask her some day.

I definitely have the impression that Beth Lamont isn't into warm cuddles and hugs. She strikes me as independent and tough.

And I admire the hell out of that attitude, even as she scares the shit out of me with how smart she is.

Chapter Three

Beth

I don't generally hate my job at the Baywater Inn. My boss isn't a prick, at least not an obvious one. I sometimes catch him checking out my ass, and he likes us to look a certain way on the job, but I suppose that comes with the territory. I guess the wealthy clientele don't like slobs serving them food, so he wants us to be neat and clean and if you happen to be a little perky, well then, added bonus. Usually.

I've heard the monthly club dues are something like ten grand. That's less than my dad's last emergency room visit but more than I make in a year. I guess if you have a lot of money, that amount isn't staggering.

My friend Abby is off tonight. I hope she's not sick. It's not like her to miss work and when she's around, work is so much more fun. She's the kind of friend whose sarcasm makes the entire day brighter. I want to text her to see if she's okay, but I'm almost over my texting limit for the month. I'll have to wait to e-mail her.

I set the dessert in the center of the table for the ladies who clearly spend their days enjoying the finer things in life. Their hands are perfectly manicured, their skin flawless. I wanted to hate these people when I first started here, but aside from a random douchebag, most of the clients are polite in a non-dickhead kind of way. Hopefully, they'll tip well today.

"Is there anything else I can get you?"

The older blonde, who doesn't look a day over thirty, shakes her head, and I leave them to tend my next table. Becky, the hostess, has seated a group of four guys at a corner table.

I start on my routine for serving a new table. I lay out the tiny drink napkins and start on the pleasantries.

"I'm Beth and I'll be taking care of you this afternoon. Can I get you started with anything from the bar?"

I scan each of the faces of the men until I get to him.

To Noah. My breath locks in my throat as our eyes collide. There's a quirk at the edge of his mouth. A cocky arrogance that was missing earlier when we were doing stats. I feel it rather than see it. My stomach tightens as the moment extends beyond recognition and into something uncomfortable and tense.

Will he point out that I'm tutoring him or will he pretend he doesn't know me?

"Hey," he says.

He's going to acknowledge me. Color me surprised. I've tutored before. Some of the guys on the basketball team and a softball player last spring. And I've encountered some of them here.

I can't explain my reaction to him. I can't control the warmth that prickles across my skin at his quiet acknowledgment.

"Nice to see you again, Noah," I manage. My voice loses its smooth edge, and I feel awkward and tense.

"Beth is tutoring me in Stats," he tells the other men. "So I don't embarrass myself and all that."

The big guy with his back to the wide bay window grins. "You were the TA in Stats last semester, weren't you?"

I remember him now with the context. Josh Douglas. He was a big guy who transferred in from another school and opted to take Stats a second time when he didn't have to. "Yes, that was me."

This is strange, this collision of two worlds. Usually there's a tacit nod or a quiet greeting, but this feels like I've been sucked into their orbit. It's not a comforting feeling because the worlds blur and along with them, the rules. I don’t want to stand here talking about stats and class when I have drinks to serve and other customers to wait on.

"Gents, what'll it be? I think we need to let Beth here get back to work." This from the thin man to my left. There is a softness to his face that contrasts sharply with the hard lines of his body.

Noah is watching me when I take their drink orders to the bar. He's sat with his back to the wall again, giving him a clear view of the hallway that leads back to the kitchen. He is the first thing I see when I come around the corner, and I notice him now, every time.

Because he is still watching for me. That is the only way to explain how his eyes happen to catch mine each time I step out of the dimly lit hallway and into his field of vision. There is a darkness there, an intensity that is both off-putting and enticing.

But there is something else there. Something that tempts me to take a single step into the darkness and let it envelop me.

It is a temptation I can't afford. A single mistake would ruin everything I have worked my ass off to achieve.

But it is a fantasy that I can indulge in if I let myself. A little fantasy never hurt anyone.

I carry the drinks to their table, pretending this is like every other table. It is a normal job. There is no need for the tension in my belly, the heat crawling across my skin. I stand between Noah and Josh now, intensely aware of Noah in a way I haven't been aware of a guy in a long time.

I go through the motions but mentally, I retreat.

There is no room in my life for this kind of fantasy stupidity.

Regardless of the warmth that unfurls in my belly and penetrates my veins.

Noah Warren is off limits.

Noah

There's something about seeing her in the crisp white shirt and black skirt that twists up my insides and reminds me that

I'm not dead and not a eunuch.

I hadn't expected to see her at the country club. 'Course I hadn't really known what I'd see at a country club. Hell, I am so far out of my league in this place, it isn't even funny. There are thousand-dollar sports coats tossed over chairs like they're ten dollar throwaways from Old Navy.

Beth moves like she fits completely in the scene. She wears comfort in her smile and competence in everything she does.

But there is something starkly feminine about her now. Something different from the cool, sexy confidence when she'd been instructing me in stats. There she'd been all business, focused on the numbers, the equations, and the work. She'd been in her flow taking me through the arguments and she'd made them sound less foreign.

I felt better about my chances of actually passing this class. And I really can't fail. It is such a freak accident that I'm even here. I will not let LT down. Failing is absolutely not an option.

Beth leans across the table to place our drinks down. She looks down at me. "Only water?"

"I'm driving," I say. The truth. My hands aren't shaking anymore from leaving the parking garage. I'm still not used to how things rise up and take over when I'm least expecting them.

My shoulder aches and I rotate it to relieve the stiffness. The pain there is a dull echo now. As long as I stay ahead of it, I'm fine.

"Okay then." She takes our orders and disappears into that dark hallway where I assume the kitchen is.

"So what's the deal with her?" Josh asks.

"She's tutoring me," I say again. Also the truth. It is so easy these days. There are fewer lies to keep track of. I can almost believe I've got my shit together.

Kind of a relief, honestly.

"Yeah? Anything else come with that service?"

I turn a hard look on Caleb. I've just met him, but decided inside of five minutes that he and I were never going to be friends. Caleb has this sense of superiority about him that used to drive me nuts about our company executive officer. The XO had to make sure everyone knew he was the smartest guy in the room and Caleb is just like that.

Guys like Caleb got people killed because they didn't listen.

"Don't be a dick."

This from Josh before I have a chance to say a word. Josh knew LT and helped get me oriented, at least to the business school.

"What? She's smoking hot. I'd tap that."

I reach for my water, briefly considering whether or not to smash the glass into Caleb's face. "We're not discussing tapping anything. We're not in Iraq anymore," I say. There's a time and a place for locker room talk, and unless I've misread the entire situation - the middle of a place like this, that drips wealth and privilege - wasn't that place.

I could be wrong, though. Judging by Josh's reaction, I don't think I am.

"So you get settled in?" Josh asks.

"Yeah. New place is nice. Perfect, actually."

"You're not living in town?" This from Nathan, who hasn't said two words since we sat down. Josh told me he was quiet. I hadn't realized how literal he'd been.

"Nah. I'm about twenty minutes from campus."

"Not taking the bus?" Nathan is still nursing his beer. Caleb has already finished his first and is now twisting in his chair, looking for Beth.

Something violent rocks through me. The idea of him thinking about her like she's some kind of fuck toy makes me physically ill.

"Hell no," I say. "I'm sure it's perfectly fine and safe, but I'll pass on mass transport, thanks."

"Don't blame you," Josh says. "Sometimes, it kills me what some of these kids think of as a prank. Some freshman threw a soda bottle full of vinegar and baking soda on one of the buses last semester. Damn near gave me a fucking heart attack."

"Nice," I say. I'm watching for Beth. I can't help it. There's something about seeing her here that makes her seem vulnerable. In class, she was all boarded up and stiff. Professional and sexy and completely off limits.

Here, she's different. Softer. More approachable. I wonder if it makes her uncomfortable knowing she can't hide behind her stern presence from class.

I want to know. I want to know why she's working here. Business school isn't generally a place where you find people who have to work their way through college.

But here she is. Delivering our food and smiling and making small talk.

My tongue is stuck. I can't think of anything blindingly brilliant to say. Instead, I watch Josh and Nathan and Caleb talk, losing myself in the warmth of her hip near my shoulder.

It's been a long time since I felt this awareness of another person. Not this kind of intense desire to know more, at any rate.

A soft touch on my shoulder. I look up to find her staring down at me. "Do you need anything else?"

Her voice is quiet, but it penetrates the fog in my brain. I shake my head. And isn't that fucking eloquent?

She walks off, and I try not to stare at the sway of her hips or the small span of her waist. She's not tiny like most of the underclassmen, but she's not an Amazon, either.

She's somewhere in between. Somewhere close to perfection.

And I'm a goddamned chump because she's made it abundantly clear that there will be no shenanigans.

Which is a shame.

Because for the first time since I've come home from the war, I feel a semblance of life in my veins. So much nicer than the haze I've been walking around in.

Pretending to live while waiting patiently to die.

Chapter Four

Beth

It's after midnight when my shift ends. I'll have to be up early. The best time to try and get through to the VA is first thing in the morning. I've never had a phone answered by a live person after ten a.m. I have no idea what they do all day, but answering the phone certainly isn't one of those things.

My feet hurt but nothing like they used to. Professor Blake gave me a gift card to Cole Haan my first year on campus. My soul had ached at the thought of spending that much money on a pair of shoes. But she'd basically ordered me not to argue because I was going to spend a lot of time on my feet. She was right. It was worth it to have a good pair of shoes beneath you.

I've had them resoled three times since she bought them for me. She was definitely right.

Still, I'm not walking home in high heels. I slide my worn sneakers on and head out into the darkness.

I don't mind walking home. I head through campus which is generally pretty safe, despite a few random incidents a few years ago.

Still, I keep a can of mace in my right hand. It might be illegal. I've never really checked, but I'm not going to be a walking statistic.

I've got too much to live for to risk it. And besides, if something happened to me, what would happen to my dad?

Headlights illuminate the dark in front of me. My blood starts pounding in my veins when I realize the car is slowing down to keep pace with me. I tighten the straps on my backpack and start scanning the area to see where I can disappear to. I'm wearing a jacket which covers my white shirt, so I'd be able to hide if I can get away from the road fast enough.

"Hey."

My stomach drops to my feet.

Noah.

"You know, it's really fucking rude to follow someone in the middle of the night." Now that I'm safe, I'm pissed. He scared the living hell out of me.

"Sorry. I just actually realized that."

He sounds genuinely embarrassed. I look down and he's leaning across the passenger's seat. "Do you want a ride?"

"You guys left hours ago," I say.

"I was curious how you were getting home."

I lift one brow. "That's a pretty lame excuse."

"Yeah well, I'm not really that smooth. What you see is what you get and all that."

He makes me want to smile, but I can't let that barrier down. Still, it's tempting to take the offered ride. It would get me home sooner. Dad might still be awake, but I doubt it. When he's like this, he sleeps on and off for days until he can walk again.

"How do I know you're not a serial killer?"

"I've got people you can call for references." He drums his fingers on the steering wheel. "Look, I was curious, okay?"

"About what?"

"You."

My breath catches in my throat. This is the strangest conversation I've had in ages. I don't have a ton of practice at this whole flirting thing, if that's what this is. I've usually got way too many things on my mind to worry about hormones. "Well, I'm sure the details of my life are incredibly boring and mundane. I think you'd be better off looking at the eligible underclassmen."

"I wasn't asking you to get married," he says. There's that crook at the corner of his mouth again. It suggests there might be dimples if he smiled. "Do you want a ride home, or are you content to skulk through campus in the dark?"

I can admit that I'm tempted. There's something rugged about Noah. An edge. There's something about him that doesn't fit into the neat caricatures of business school students.

I'm hesitating. There is frustration in the lines around his mouth, but I'm not really keen on him knowing where I live. I can't explain it, but I don't want him to see the tiny two-bedroom house that I share with my dad.

My dad gave up everything for me to go to school here. I shouldn't be ashamed that we're scraping by, but I am.

"Hello?" He waves his hand to get my attention.

"No funny business?"

"Hand to God," he says.

I get in the car.

"Nice ride." It seems like a safe conversation piece.

Another thing about him that doesn't fit the business school stereotype. His car is clean and taken care of, without demonstrating that obsessive cleanliness and shine of people who have way too much identity based on the vehicle they drive. It is also not nice enough to be doubling as an exoskeleton for his penis. For some reason, that makes me relax a little more around him.

"Thanks. I bought it when I first joined the army. Even managed not to get screwed on the interest rate."

I look over at him. The pale blue lights from the dashboard cut harsh angles into his cheeks. "That's impressive. I thought all car dealers around military installations were criminal."

He looks over at me, curiosity in his dark eyes.

"How do you know about car dealerships around military bases?"

"My dad used to be in the army," I admit, and I instantly regret mentioning the military bases. I don't want to talk about the army with him.

"Really? Where was he stationed?"

"He was at Fort Benning before he got out."

"I never served at Benning. My first duty station was Fort

Hood, in Texas," he says. "I hear Columbus is nice, though."

"It's certainly better than Fayetteville and Fort Bragg."

"Bragg was my last duty station. I've got a lot of friends down there."

"Were you Airborne?" I can't help it. My dad's certificate from Airborne school still hangs on the wall in his room. I thought it would remind him of the good times. I don't think he's ever noticed that it's there. I notice it though. Every time I bring him his medication, the plaques and certificates I hung for him taunt me with the man he used to be. They are a reminder of everything he gave up so I could be where I am.

Noah

She is sitting quietly now. No longer Beth the tutor or Beth the waitress. No, this is a new aspect of Beth. So many facets to her. She is fascinating and I'm enjoying the sensation of her getting underneath my skin.

I honestly didn't think she was going to get in the car and I don't really have a good excuse for going back to the country club and checking on her. We'd stayed for hours, drinking and reminiscing about our former lives. War stories always felt good when you were with people who understood the life you'd lived.

It was such a far cry from sitting in classes with kids whose closest experience with war is Call of Duty.

"Why did you get out?" she asks after a long silence. We're sitting at a stoplight.

Such a loaded, simple question. I breathe deeply for a minute, trying to figure out how much to tell her. I don't want to look at her and see pity looking back at me. So many people look at those of us who join the military as a bunch of mouth-breathing idiots who couldn't do anything else with our lives.

She doesn't strike me as the judgmental type, but I can't know for sure. And I don't want to spoil the moment by letting my own bitterness and stereotypes into the conversation.

"My contract was up. I served with a buddy who pushed

me to apply to the business school and well, here I am."

"Were you an officer?"

I shake my head. "No. I was enlisted. Got out as a staff sergeant."

She frowns at me. "How long were you in?"

"A little under five years."

"Wasn't that a little fast?"

I shrug. She clearly knows more about the military than most military brats. "A little," I admit. "But we were - are - at war. We tend to promote anyone with a pulse to fill the rosters."

She doesn't think my joke is funny. It's actually a pretty shitty joke, one that usually only other soldiers get, and it usually prompts another round of commiserating on how fucked up the entire mission was and still is.

"So you ended up here," she says.

"Yep. Hit the lottery in a lot of ways. It definitely takes some getting used to." I roll to a stop at another light. We're off campus now. "Where am I taking you?"

She directs me to her address. We turn down well-lit streets. It's in a nicer part of town close to campus. The houses are neat if small. They look old and well restored. Impressive, really. There's a lot of money at this school.

Which makes her job at the country club that much more interesting. If she lives in a swanky part of town, what's she doing with a job?

"So I wanted to say thanks for taking me on with the whole tutoring thing," I say. I want to put her at ease. She looks tense. Awkward. I'm not sure what to do to help her relax.

"No problem. We'll keep your GPA up."

I grin. I can't help it. "I'm not worried about how high my GPA is. I'm more concerned with failing."

"You won't fail." There's an edge to her words, an undercurrent of steel that surprises me.

"Don't underestimate how much my brain resists math."

She smiles, and it transforms her. She's exhausted, but her face softens in the low light. "Don't underestimate my ability to teach."

"I guess I'll have to have faith then, won't I?"

"Faith, no. Practice, yes. Take the next right then I'm the second house on the left."

I turn down the street and stop where she tells me.

"Thank you for the ride," she says. "I appreciate it."

"No problem." I hesitate for a moment. "You don't have a car?"

"I like to walk. Gets me outside."

She's not lying, but she's not telling the entire truth, either. Her story doesn't jive with the neighborhood that she lives in. I'm used to watching my soldiers and figuring out when they're lying to me.

I'm not going to call her on it. Because nothing says *stalker* like "I can tell you're lying to me" in the first twenty-four hours of meeting someone.

"I'll see you in class." She unfolds her long legs out of the car. She's not wearing those glorious heels she had on earlier. It's a shame because she's got amazing legs, and those heels made them go on and on forever.

I watch her climb the steps for a moment, then pull away before she goes inside. I figure I've been enough of a psycho for one night.

But my curiosity about Beth hasn't really been satisfied. If anything, I've got more questions. She's so unlike most of the females around here. Hell, she's not like most of the males, either.

As much as I hate stats, I can't wait for our next class. Stats might just become my favorite subject.

Chapter Five

Beth

I wait until Noah pulls away then jogged off the steps and down the street toward my house. I haven't been too far off with the address I gave him. It belonged to a little old lady who was recently put into a home. I used to stop by and drop off her medications. Another odd job I'd done to earn extra money on the side. I missed Ellie sometimes.

It's really amazing how three streets over can go from being in the nice part of town to being in one of the sketchier parts. I don't want to make our neighborhood sound like it's some violent, trash-ridden dump. It isn't. Our neighbors are all working class and everyone looks out for each other in the vague way that people who work on different shifts do. We know who belongs and who doesn't.

But compared to the street where Noah dropped me off, our neighborhood feels...abused.

Still, it's home. It isn't perfect, but I have my dad and I am going to school and, you know, sometimes being a little hungry isn't a bad thing.

I let myself into our house. I really need to remember to pick up some WD-40 the next time Dad's check comes in. The door creaks something terrible.

The light from the TV casts an eerie glow in the small living room. The threadbare rug is a score I'd found in a dumpster behind one of the houses that are not officially fraternities, but everyone knows exactly what they are. That was before Dad's back had taken a turn for the worse and the VA had demonstrated just how completely fucked up they are. It was right around the same time that I'd gotten a healthy dose of just what "not 100-percent disabled" meant financially.

My blood pressure rises just thinking about the nightmare of phone calls I will have to contend with again tomorrow. My dad needs an injection in his back but because the powers that be judged them as elective, we've either got to get them done at the VA or pay out of pocket. And we can't afford them out of pocket.

But right now, I slip into the living room. Dad is laid out on the couch but at least he's awake. He offers a blurry kind of smile. "Hey, sugar bear."

I lean down to kiss his cheek. "Hi, Dad. How's your back?"

"Been worse, I suppose."

He's wearing one shoe. It's not laced up and it's half off his heel. "How did you get that on?" I don't care that he's gotten up - that is a good thing. But it hurts him to put his shoes on when his back is out.

"I had to try and see if I was still completely useless." He glances down at the single shoe. "I sneezed when I was bent over and damn near blacked out from the pain."

"Ah hell, Dad." My heart gets a little tighter in my chest. I lean against the edge of the couch and ease the shoe off his foot. He used to be so active, so alive.

So different from the man who can barely get off the couch.

I keep telling myself this is just temporary, that I'll get a job that has insurance and I'll claim him as my dependent. I'll get him the best back doc in the country and he'll get fixed.

My eyes burn because it is such a far-off goal. It feels like more of a dream. We barely have enough money for his prescriptions. The idea that someday I'll have a job where I make enough money to have insurance, too, is...sometimes it feels like a fantasy that people like me live on, just to keep going.

I pull his one sock off and drop it on the floor by his shoes. "Want some help up?"

He shakes his head, his eyes closed. "I'm going to sleep out here tonight, I think."

"I'll get the heating pad. Did you get your evening medicine?"

His words are blurred together, jumbled. "I doubled up after the sneezing incident. I'm out until the VA can see me again for a refill."

"Crap. You are supposed to have enough to get you through to Wednesday." My stomach twists. I don't know what the kind of pain my father lives with feels like, but I know what seeing him in it does to me.

There is no way he's moving tomorrow.

I fight back tears as I check the cabinet where we keep the alcohol. I'm not much of a drinker. Dad doesn't really have a problem with it, despite me being underage. I don't drink that often, though, because what if I drink and he needs it?

We have a half-gallon of vodka. It's going to be close. I don't know if that will hold him for two days or not but he'll need it in the morning after his medication wears off.

The first time he ran out of medication after he'd gotten out of the army, I discovered how to get him through between appointments. It involves me buying alcohol with a fake ID and him getting hammered until he can't stand up.

Guess chipped discs in your spine will do that to a guy.

I hate seeing him drunk, but it's infinitely better than seeing him in pain.

I only had to clean up pee once, when he'd thought he was in the bathroom and instead had been in the kitchen.

I am so tired. All I want to do is sleep for one night without worrying about whether my dad is going to be able to move in the morning. Without worrying how we are going to pay the bills. Or whether we are going to have food in the house.

I blink hard. I have papers to grade, but I'll do it tomorrow. I just need to sleep before my dad sees me crying. I can't let him see me cry.

I cover him with a blanket and kiss him on the forehead.

"Love you, sugar bear."

"Love you, too, Dad."

My voice doesn't break. Barely. It's only when I'm down the hall and my door is closed that I let the tears come. They burn down my cheeks and relieve some of the pressure around my heart.

But they do nothing to ease the growing frustration that no matter how much I do, it is never enough.

Noah

I'm renting a small house outside of town. It's not exactly country living but it damn sure isn't living crammed into the city like the neighborhood where Beth lives. It isn't much, but it is home for the time being.

And hell, it beats being in Iraq.

The kitchen sink still has remnants of breakfast. Guess the dishes aren't going to wash themselves. I can't ignore the four orange pill bottles lined up like sentries in the open cabinet near the kitchen sink. I reach for the one farthest to the left.

Princess Ambien and I had become lovers before I left Iraq, and she's never left me alone and afraid in the dark. I sleep like a champ with her. I don't know how people do it without her. She'll give me a few minutes to take a shower and all that, but soon she'll reach up and tug me to bed. Tuck herself around me like a warm blanket and pull me down into a mostly dreamless sleep.

It isn't the life I dreamt of for myself, but if the worst thing that happens to me from Iraq is that I need a little help sleeping, I figure I've come out ahead of most.

I shower and dry off, sliding between the cool sheets. They're scratchy tonight. My skin is tight, my hands dry.

I stare at the moonlight that spills into my bedroom. You can actually see the moon up in the sky out here away from the city lights. And the stars. I couldn't see them in Iraq. Too much dust in the city.

Tonight, though, I stare at the moonlight, and I think

about Beth.

Her mouth in a firm line when she's in class. All business and proper.

Her mouth as she asked us what we wanted to drink. Softer. Smoother. Friendlier. That's what it was. She was friendlier at the country club.

I guess it has to do with tips and all that. Can't count on good tips if your customers don't think you're warm and charming.

It's a toss-up which Beth I'm thinking about. The two images blur as Princess Ambien slips her arms around my waist and pulls me gently toward sleep.

The last thing I remember is her standing on the porch of her house, waiting for me to drive off.

I wonder if she'll let me give her a ride home tomorrow.

Chapter Six

Beth

"No, I'm sorry, that's not acceptable." My voice is shrill. Almost breaking. "You can't do this. He's out of medication. He's in pain."

"Miss, I'm sorry but he's going to have to wait to see his doctor. If the pain gets too bad, bring him to the emergency room."

My face is burning hot. I'm fighting the urge to start screaming. "What happened to his appointment?" It's the fifth time I've asked this question of three different people.

The answers are all different. It doesn't matter because the end result is the same.

My dad's appointment has been canceled, and without a new appointment, they won't issue him new medication because he's on heavy narcotics.

"I need to speak with a supervisor."

"Miss, she's gone to lunch. I can have her call you back."

"Then find me someone else to talk to!" My ability to remain polite is fraying at the edges. On some rational level, I realize that none of this is the fault of the woman on the other end of the phone, but I don't really care about that at this moment.

The line goes quiet, and for a moment, I think she's hung up on me. It wouldn't be the first time for that, either.

I'm pretty sure I hate the VA. I'm sure the people there are lovely at Christmas and holidays, and at some point, they actually mean well. But I've been fighting this system for years, and I've lost any charitable feelings toward anyone in that agency.

"Miss Lamont, your father's appointment has been rescheduled."

"For when?" The words are a snarl.

We live six miles from the VA. I can take the city bus and be there in thirty minutes. I could drive, but it takes as long to find parking as it does to take the bus. I can find a real person and maybe, just maybe, find a piece of humanity in this terrible monster of a bureaucratic nightmare.

"Next Tuesday."

"And what's he supposed to do in the meantime?"

"He can come into the emergency room and we can get him a prescription to cover him until then."

This does nothing to soothe my anger, but I don't have a choice. It's better than nothing because the last time they canceled his appointment, he was out of medication for almost a month.

And we ran out of money well before the end of the month because vodka, even cheap vodka, costs more than I made in tips that month.

I somehow manage to thank her and write down the appointment information.

I try to wake my dad. He's staring at the TV in some kind of trance. He's not asleep, but he's definitely not hearing me. This sometimes happens. It's like he goes away, and I can't reach him.

It scared me the first time it happened.

"Dad." I shake his shoulder hard, jarring him out of it.

"Hey, sugar bear." His words are slurred. He's halfway in the bottle. He had to get up today and go to the bathroom. He fell trying to get off the toilet.

I hate the war. I hate the army. I hate the VA.

I'm going to fix this.

Goddamn it, I'm going to fix this.

"Dad, I've got an appointment for next week. You need to stop drinking so I can take you to the emergency room when I get home, okay?"

He nods. I hope he actually heard me. He knows this drill all too well but only if I've managed to get through the alcohol haze. We tried to take him in once when I was sixteen and he'd been intoxicated. They'd called the state and tried to take me away from him. He'd been out of the army by then, but we were still in Columbus. I'd called his old brigade commander and thankfully he'd helped get things sorted out.

There was no one here to call to sort things out. We weren't at risk of me getting taken away anymore. No, it was worse. Dad needed to be sober when I took him to the ER; otherwise there would be no new medication.

It was a goddamned catch-22. He could drink to manage the pain, but he couldn't get more pain meds. But in order to get the pain meds, he had to be in pain and stone sober.

I move the vodka away from him. I trust him, but there is no reason to tempt Murphy and all that.

I'm still pissed as I leave the house and head to campus. I'm not in the mood for business ethics today. I don't want to be around anyone.

I want to sit in my room and sleep. Maybe have a good cry.

But I can't.

Because I've got class.

And my father's life depends on me getting this damned degree.

Noah

Business ethics" is kind of like "military intelligence." An oxymoron at best. How the hell can you combine ethics with profit when money undermines everything? But it's required as part of my degree program, and I figure it can't be that terrible of a class.

Josh sits down next to me. "Good times, huh? I wonder if this will be like one of those "don't beat your wife" safety briefings. Here's how not to get in trouble running your business."

I grin, trying to hide my discomfort. My hands are unsteady this morning. The anxiety meds haven't kicked in. Either that or I need a stronger dose. My stomach is in knots, and I slept like shit. Apparently I'm developing a tolerance to Princess Ambien and isn't *that* a thought that's loaded with discomfort. Add in that I wasn't able to sit at the back of the classroom. There's an Asian girl behind me writing in her notebook. I can hear the scratch of her pen against the paper. It might as well be a nail file against sandpaper.

But when Beth walks through the door, my whole perspective shifts. The scratching of the pen behind me fades. For a moment, I'm over the moon that she's in this class, too, but then I notice her eyes.

They're red, along with the tip of her nose. She's been crying.

I hate to think of her crying. It does something terrible to my heart that she's upset about something.

I stand up and get ready to ask her if she's okay. She sees me and offers a half-assed nod of acknowledgment.

And lucky for me, the only other empty seat in the class is next to mine.

I couldn't have planned it better. I guess having the scratching pen behind me is worth it if Beth gets to sit next to me.

"Rough night?" I ask when she slides into the chair.

"You could say that." Her voice is broken, rough. Like she's spent the night in a smoky bar.

"Anything I can do?"

"Do you happen to have a stash of Oxycodone around that you'd let me buy?"

I look at her hard then. That was not the response I expected. It hits me like a wet towel. I open my mouth to speak, but she beats me to it.

"Sorry, bad joke."

"Are you sick?"

She shakes her head as the professor walks in. He's a skinny man that reminds me of a ferret. He's got a pinched face and quick brown eyes that scan the room. He reminds me of my old company first sergeant. Mean old bastard but damn good in a firefight. It's not fair, but I'm not feeling charitable at the moment, even with Beth sitting next to me. Then again, some of the men I served with didn't radiate competence and character either. So I'm not sure why I expect bastions of virtue and honor in academia.

"So today's discussion is going to focus on the reading from the first assignment."

There is a groan through the class. Apparently, I'm not the only one who failed to check the syllabus.

"We're going to start the module on moral decision making with a thought experiment. There's a trolley speeding down a track. The brakes are out. On one track, there is a single person. On the other, a group of five construction workers. There is a switch that, if thrown, will go to either the left or the right. How do you decide who dies?"

A hand shoots up in the front of the class. The person attached to that hand is smooth and polished. She looks like a Ralph Lauren photo advertisement. "It's a no-brainer. You flip the switch and take out the one."

"Why?"

The poster child looks confused. "Why what?"

"Why do you choose one instead of five, Parker?" Apparently Professor Earl has spent some time memorizing our names. Which is actually impressive on a couple of different levels.

Parker frowns, and I think it might be the first time she's ever had to think hard about a response. "Because losing one person is better than losing five," she says, but she's no longer confident.

The professor continues. "The trolley experiment is meant to get us thinking about utilitarian judgments and the challenges associated with that decision-making framework. What if the one individual was Mother Teresa and the five were convicted murderers? Does that change the decision?"

Parker the poster girl doesn't raise her hand. Beside me,

Josh shifts uncomfortably. I'm not too thrilled with this question either. These aren't sterile thought experiments. This is dancing uncomfortably close to some ugly truths I'd rather forget.

I raise my hand. "It's one thing to play mental games in class. It's another to have to live with the consequences of your decision."

"Very good, Mr. Warren. What kinds of decisions do business leaders have to make and how do you adjudicate between them?"

Beth raises her hand. "The focus on profit makes it difficult to consider other factors in a business context. The medical insurance industry, for example, focuses on how to minimize patient access to care in order to maintain maximum profits. The entire bureaucracy is designed to prevent people from seeking out care. It's easier to look at the numbers on a spreadsheet than to think about how those five murderers' families will feel if they're sacrificed to save the life of a saint."

There is an edge in her words, a barely restrained fury lacing each word. Is this what had her upset before class? But she should have medical insurance through the school - most students do.

"So then how do you propose businesses make decisions?" This from Poster Girl Parker, who's twists in her chair to look back at Beth. "The consequentialist moral framework costs too much money."

"So we're putting prices on human life," Beth says. The edge is still there. Violence simmering just below the surface. "If that's what we're willing to do when we make business decisions, that's fine; but we need to acknowledge that's what we're actually doing."

I'm fascinated by the passion in her words. Like she's standing at the front of a column of advancing warriors, ready to defend the realm.

Her cheeks flush as she speaks and there's a light in her eyes. She's transformed from Beth the college student to Beth the Valkyrie. Both are equally stunning. I'm enthralled by her vehemence.

I am beyond screwed. Because I can no longer see her as merely my tutor.

She is a craving, sliding through my veins and making me want more.

Chapter Seven

Beth

I leave the classroom as soon as possible. I have to get away. The air is crushing me. The ethics class has fired me up and not in a good way. I was already wound up from the phone calls this morning, and arguing ethical dilemmas struck a nerve that I wasn't prepared for.

Sitting next to Noah threw me off balance and my comment to him about Oxy snuck out before I even knew what I was saying. It is universally stupid to even joke about stuff like that. I don't know him well enough, and it isn't something I joke about with anyone. Because the reality is about as unfunny as it comes.

"Beth!"

I try to pretend I haven't heard him, but he catches up too quickly with those long legs of his. "Hey, wait up a sec."

I stop and close my eyes, searching for some semblance of professionalism. I need my mask back in place, and I need it now. I'm feeling far too exposed today. Raw from dealing with the VA and, if I am honest with myself, a little afraid.

My dad is getting worse. The last time he threw his back out, he was flat out for a month. This time, it's been close to three, and the VA docs are no closer to getting him fixed than they were when this process started.

I stiffen when Noah's hand closes over my shoulder. His touch is strong and solid and offers a comfort that is far too tempting. He stands a little too close, his hand warm where he touches me. There is strength there. Real. It is a comfort that I badly need and for a moment, I allow myself to be selfish and don't pull away.

"Are you okay?"

Genuine concern in his words. Noah is nothing like I expected a former soldier to be – nothing like my dad's friends before he got hurt. They used to come to the house and drink and play cards and talk endless amounts of trash. If not for that stupid bravado, my dad might not have gone on his last Airborne jump. He might not have destroyed his back trying to prove he was still high speed and low drag.

Noah is nothing like the men my father used to call friends. There is no arrogant bravado, no need to cross the line between hoah and stupid. He is...he is just a good guy.

"Some girl is going to be really lucky to land you." My words slip out before I can stop them.

"I think that's a compliment?" He flushes and drags his hand through his hair. It makes me like him a little more. "But you avoided the question."

I look away then, because the concern in his eyes is blinding. "Just a rough morning," I say. Because I cannot find the words to tell him how tired I really am.

Because he is not mine to lean on. Not like that anyway. I'm his stats tutor, and there can be nothing else. No one wants to compete with a girl's father for her attention.

Every one of my relationships in the past ended because of my dad. And I'm better off without them, but I'm also tired of the heartbreak. I don't have the energy to deal with it anymore.

"Rough enough that you were crying before class."

Damn, he saw that. "What are you?" I ask, cracking a half smile. "Most guys don't notice anything beyond the size of a girl's tits, and you're actually telling me you noticed I'd been crying?"

He returns the half-assed grin. "Well, I mean, I did notice your, ahem, curves, but seeing how I've developed a thing for your eyes, I noticed those, too."

"My eyes, huh? That's not a euphemism?"

His thumb brushes my shoulder. I can feel the gesture

beneath my sweater. I resist the urge to lean into the caress. "It depends," he says. "Do you want it to be?"

I smile and shake my head. "Thanks for that. I needed a laugh."

"You didn't really laugh. You just kind of smiled sadly."

He steps closer until I can feel the heat radiating from his body. He's wearing a light blue striped button-down shirt and black pants. He looks every bit the business school student. It's his hands, though, that give him away. They're rough. Not manicured like many of the business school upperclassmen.

"My life is kind of a disaster, that's all." I want so badly to lean on him. To pretend that I could lay all of my problems in his lap, and he'd just hold me while I talked to him.

It's a stupid fantasy. The world doesn't work that way for girls like me. I'm not quite from the wrong side of the tracks, but I don't fit in with the women here who come from money and are looking for a husband with the right pedigree.

No, for women like me, the story is dramatically different. It usually involves a cat or six, and many beloved nieces and nephews if we have siblings.

Since I have neither, I'm leaning toward cats. Except that cats cost money, and we can't really afford another mouth to feed at the moment. Maybe when I get insurance.

"Want to get some coffee and tell me about it?"

My stomach takes that moment to rumble. Loudly. I want to crawl into a hole and die because Noah looks down in the vicinity of my belly. "Or I can buy you lunch."

"You don't need to buy me lunch," I say. But there's not much protest in my voice because I'm not prone to lying to myself or others. I am hungry. The apple and yogurt I'd had for breakfast didn't hold me over very long.

"I'd like to." His hand is still on my shoulder.

There are a hundred different reasons why I shouldn't go to lunch with him. Why I should go finish my assignments for the week and get prepared for our next tutoring session. I've got four more hours before Dad should be sober enough to take to the emergency room.

There are so many things I should be doing instead of going to lunch, but for one blindingly stupid moment, I want nothing more than to be normal.

And so I let my stupid need not to be alone take the lead. I nod and offer a warm smile. "That would be nice."

Noah

The mystery that is Beth Lamont continues to deepen. I half expected her to say no. The redness in her eyes is gone now, but the fatigue is still there.

"Where would you like to eat?"

"Whatever's easiest," she says.

"You're going to have to help me out here. I'm not over the getting-lost-on campus part of this operation." But she doesn't smile so I pull out my phone and look up local restaurants nearby.

She falls into step next to me, which is good because I have the strongest desire to pull her into a hug. She looks like she's about to fall over. I've seen people look like she does. Coming off of long ruck marches, they do everything they can to stay upright, but the march has taken every ounce of energy they've got. They either sit down on their own or they collapse.

I'm hoping she'll make it to my car before she crumbles.

"So what led to the rough morning? Fight with the doctors?"

She sucks in a quick breath. It's subtle, but I notice because I notice everything about her. She's more pale than normal.

"Something like that," she says.

"Are you sick?"

"No." Her response is quick. A little too quick.

"Family?"

A quiet sigh. "My dad."

We enter the parking garage, and she follows me up the deadly stairwell to the second floor where my car is. I'm good at hiding it. I fucking hate parking garages. The stairs, man, the stairs are a fatal funnel. There's no defending yourself. One disciplined shooter can control the entire approach.

I pause at the top of the steps, looking into the cavernous parking garage. I'm not insane enough to think there's actual danger lurking in the shadows, but try telling that to my nervous system that reacts to every parking garage like I'm back in Iraq. I'm paranoid enough that I'm alert to the possibilities. Criminals tend to seek out the weak, and at approaching six feet tall, I'm not weak. But I'm also unable to relax.

Beth's hand is gentle and strong on my upper back. "Hey, where'd you go just then?"

I try to shake off the question. "My PTSD flares up in parking garages. Just checking to make sure there're no bad guys hiding in the dark."

She makes a sound that's somewhere between skeptical and amused. "That explains why you checked on me when I was walking home," she says.

"Bad guys like to hide in the dark," is all I manage. She's caught me, but I'm not sure if she realizes that she's seen a good chunk that remains wrong with me.

I've come home from the war pretty normal, all things considered. I'm dealing with the anxiety and the sleep problems. I'm actually considering trying to get my doc to wean me off the pain meds for my shoulder, but I'm going to hold off until after the fall semester. I don't want to be dealing with pain and trying to pass Stats. I've got more than enough to worry about without adding to the chaos of my first year as a civilian.

"Some of the worst of the worst, though, are hiding in broad daylight," she says as she climbs into the passenger's seat.

"True enough," I say. My throat is dry. Goddamn it I hate the parking garage. "How hard is it to get a parking pass somewhere else on campus?"

"Depends on how much money you've got lying around. Why not take the bus?"

I pause, taking my hand off the shifter where I was going to put the car in reverse. I twist toward her, wanting to get closer. "You know that whole parking garage issue I've got? I'm worse about busses."

"Fair enough. You could park off campus and walk in, though."

"How far?"

"Not too far. I usually walk to campus each day. There're lots of places just off campus you can park for a small daily fee. It's probably cheaper than parking in here every day anyway."

A half-assed idea forms and it escapes before I think better of it. "I could park at your house and walk you to class every day."

"But then I'd have to explain you to my dad, and he's made me swear off boys until I graduate from grad school."

"Seriously?" I'm suddenly really curious about this mysterious father of hers. He's sick but dictating her life…

"I'm kidding, Noah," she whispers.

I'm struck by the sound of my name on her lips. It's something smooth and sensual and my mind detours into a decidedly not comforting place. "That's the first time you've said my name." I like it. A lot more than I probably should.

It was a whisper across her lips. I want to hear her say it again. I suddenly want very much to see if she'd let me kiss her. I wasn't lying when I told her I had a thing for her eyes. The green is intense and lined with grey but it's her mouth that draws me closer. It's wide and full and the perfect shade of pink against her skin.

I sound like a romantic, and maybe the war has made me appreciate beautiful things. There's not a lot of beauty at war. Terrible things. Ugly things. Anything good ends up destroyed. Violently.

She hasn't moved since I spoke. Silent and still, she's so quiet I can hear her breathing. "I've said your name before." A hushed whisper.

"No, I'd remember." I'm closer now. Close enough that I can feel the heat from her skin, the quiet huff of her breath against my mouth.

This could ruin everything. If I'm wrong, she could run out of my car, and I would have to let her go.

But I lean a little closer. Until my lips brush against hers. She's so much softer than I imagined. I nudge her gently, searching for permission before I go any further.

Her lips part, and then I'm not thinking anymore. I'm feeling. The soft glide of her tongue. The warm press of her lips against mine. The mingling of breath until I can't tell where she ends and I begin.

My hand shakes as I slide my palm over her cheek, cupping her face gently. Her skin is soft, so soft compared to the hard calluses on mine.

And I kiss her like she's my first taste of salvation.

Because she is. She just doesn't know it yet.

Chapter Eight

Beth

I won't say that kissing Noah is a mistake. It is a breath of something beautiful in the dark fatigue of my life. I love the feel of his mouth on mine, his taste. He's spicy, like cinnamon mixed with citrus. Warm and clean and fresh and a thousand other things that are pure and good.

The kiss ends after a moment. It could have been me, maybe him. I can't tell. He rests his forehead against mine, and we sit there silently, simply trying to catch our breath.

"I'm not sure what to say," I finally manage, giving voice to the thoughts swirling inside me.

There are darker thoughts. Ones that involve the slide of skin against skin, the fantasy of having time only to myself.

"Me, either." A gentle brush of his lips against mine. "Still hungry?"

"Starved." Not only for food, but I'm sure he's already figured that out. I want to kiss him again already.

I wish I were more creative. I might suggest some wild double entendre. Make him laugh. But I'm not that good.

He releases me, and I sink back into my seat. He drives us out of the parking garage and heads off campus, checking his phone for directions. I want to ask where he's taking us, but I'm willing to let him surprise me. Because I'm living dangerously, right? Being selfish for one fleeting moment.

"So what's wrong with your dad?" He's heading into the nice part of town. The *really* nice part of town that has all the great local restaurants that I've heard my classmates talk about.

There's a social aspect of business school that I know is hurting my chances of getting into graduate school. It's part of why I'm not even sure about applying. The social scene is something I have neither the time nor the resources to participate in. I'm counting on a recommendation from Professor Blake because I damn sure haven't made the contacts that I should have been making. And I don't think we can afford it.

Which isn't to say I don't have friends. I do. But I shelter my life from them. The clothes I wear are from the secondhand shops in the wealthier parts of town. I look like I belong, or at least I try to convince myself that I look like I fit. I have Abby to thank for teaching me how to pass here.

I have no idea what's being said behind my back, and if I spend too much time thinking about it, I'll go crazy. I focus on my grades and my work. Everything else can't matter.

"He got hurt in the army. He's got two herniated discs in his mid-back."

"My first platoon sergeant had something similar. Screwed it up on a jump." He pulls into a parking spot in front of a brightly colored Mexican restaurant. "Do you like Mexican?"

"It's my favorite." The truth. It isn't expensive to make at home, and usually at the first of the month when Dad's check comes in, I buy and freeze fresh ingredients to use throughout the month. Some months, depending on the medications my dad is running low on, are better than others.

My stomach is clearly in the mood for Mexican. I still have time before Dad will be sober. It's kind of pathetic that I know how long it takes. Part of me feels like I'm enabling him but what else are we supposed to do?

I'll drive him to the ER and they'll give him some medication that will make him okay until the follow-up appointment. Sometimes, there's a steroid injection they can do that works miracles but it isn't often. Some docs disagree about whether or not they're necessary or if they're making things worse. It's not the real injection he needs anyway. Just a temporary fix, but so long as he's sober, the ER will treat him, as opposed to diagnose him as an addict and refuse to prescribe. It's another medical bill to add to the pile, but he won't be in pain for a little while and that's what matters.

It's a sad state of affairs but that's my life, right?

Noah holds the door for me as we step inside. His hand drifts to the small of my back. It's warm and solid and comforting. He asks for a small table away from the high traffic areas. I've noticed that about him: he always sits with his back to the wall. Part of me wants to ask about it; part of me doesn't want to put him on the spot.

I figure if he wants to talk about it, he will.

Right now, I am going to enjoy lunch. Lunch with Noah. A completely impractical escape from reality. Lunch can't hurt anything, right?

The echo of his mouth on mine, the warmth of his touch tingles on my lips.

Heat crawls across my skin as I lower my hand. He's watching me. His eyes darken as he watches me. Warmth slides through my veins. His gaze drops to my lips then slips back over my face. I've never felt caressed by a simple look before but there's something about the way he watches me.

"I would really like to kiss you again, sometime," he murmurs after our waiter leaves.

I sip my water, desperate for a distraction. Not because I don't want to kiss him again, but because I do. Because the man sitting across from me with the rough, gentle hands is such a complex variation from the guys I deal with every day. He's been out in the world. He's really lived; he's gone to war. He's done so much more than just being a college student.

And while I want to pretend that this might be something different, I'm wary. I've been burned before. My hormones might be all "hurray for penis" but my brain knows better than to jump into bed with the first guy in a long time who gets me a little stirred up.

Then again, he's only said he wants to kiss me again. That doesn't automatically mean we're going to be getting hot and sweaty any time soon.

"You know you could say something," he says. "Your

silence is hell on the ego. Did I have bad breath?"

He catches me off guard. I laugh and it feels good. "No. Sorry. Lost in thought."

"Good ones or...?"

Because I can't help myself, I meet his eyes. Warmth looks back at me. He covers one of my hands with his. "You've definitely made the day a little brighter," I say.

He strokes his thumb along mine, sending little shivers of pleasure across my skin. "That's good to know. I'll have to come up with other ways to make your day a little brighter."

I shake my head. "Another euphemism?"

"Maybe. Though clearly I need to work on them."

We sit there talking about nothing and everything. About classes and how the basketball team won their last game and nonsensical things that don't matter. It's a completely normal afternoon in my abnormal life.

The whole time, his hand covers mine, his thumb stroking slowly. A light, teasing caress. No pressure. Just…connection. A human touch when I wasn't looking for anything but a paycheck.

It looks like I've gotten way more than I bargained for.

Noah

"So your dad. Why hasn't he been seen at the VA?"

She leans back as the waiter brings us chips and salsa and our drinks. She dips a chip and takes a bite. She's stalling, but I'm not sure why.

"We should try to keep this conversation light and enjoyable. If you get me started on the VA, I may start using creative profanity."

I lean a little closer so I can whisper in her ear. I'm tempted to bite her earlobe but I'm trying to behave. My restraint is damn near superhuman "I'm dying to hear what you consider creative profanity. I can't picture you swearing."

"The VA is one of the few institutions that gets my blood pressure up that high."

"Why?" I haven't been seen by the VA yet. I'm still on Tricare for a few more weeks and then I'm taking advantage of the student insurance. I've heard enough horror stories about the VA that make me skeptical at best. I won't be able to avoid it forever, especially not with everything that happened to me during the war. But I'm content to avoid it for now.

Beth sips her water then takes a deep breath. "They cancel more appointments than they keep, and he's been scheduled for surgery five times in the last year. Because he's not 100-percent disabled, he doesn't have full coverage at local hospitals. And because of his rating, his back problems are treated as elective as opposed to medically necessary." She takes a deep breath. Her voice is laced with tension. "It's complicated."

"Shit, I'm sorry."

"Thanks." She snags another chip. "So what's your story? You're a junior?"

"I took a lot of courses after work when I was down at Bragg. School accepted most of my transfer credits. I get to use my GI Bill to finish up my BA and then I'm applying to grad school."

"My dad gave me his GI Bill," she says after a moment. "He's the reason I can even begin to afford to go here."

There's something else there, beneath her words but I don't push her on it. "I'm glad I went to school while I was active."

"How did you have time? If you got promoted so quickly you had to be working a lot."

"I was, but I carved out time. I didn't know what I wanted to be when I grew up so I joined the army."

"You joined the army on a whim during war?" Her words are laced with sarcasm.

I laugh and almost choke on a chip. How's that for romantic? Smooth, Noah, real smooth. "When you put it that way, it does sound kind of foolish," I say when I'm done hacking up a lung.

"I don't know too many people who would join the army because they didn't know what they wanted to be when they grow up. A couple of guys I went to high school with joined because they wanted to blow stuff up or because their dads wanted them to."

She's avoiding my eyes now, but she hasn't pulled her hand from beneath mine. I hope she doesn't feel the tremble in my hand. The anxiety is back, squeezing my lungs. Making me want to retreat into the shadows and comfort of the medication. Anything to take the edge off. I consider ordering a beer to get me through the rest of the day, but I don't make it a habit of drinking and driving.

No, my other vices are plenty. No need to add criminal offenses to my list of sins in this life.

"How did that turn out for them?" I ask.

"I don't know. My dad moved with me here once I got accepted, so I lost touch with a lot of people from high school."

"You don't sound like it's much of a loss."

She shrugs, swirling her tortilla chip in the salsa. Her hand tightens beneath mine. "I've always had a hard time fitting in."

"You seem like you're passing pretty well here. The professors like you."

"The professors continually tell me they've never had a student work like me. And I'm not sure if it's a compliment or not," she says.

"Why wouldn't it be?"

"Maybe my working too hard makes my class background obvious." She rolls her eyes with a funny smile on her lips. "Like my freshman year, my friend Abby pulled me aside and basically said, 'I'm your fairy godmother. Here's how you pretend you belong here just like the rest of them'."

It's so strange, hearing her talk about how she doesn't fit. I never would have figured that she feels this way. It's true enough that she's working and she walks everywhere but the way she carries herself makes me think quiet sophistication. The mystery of Beth Lamont deepens and I want to know more. So much more.

She catches me watching her and flushes. I love the way her cheeks turn a little bit pink, matching the tone of her lips.

"Sorry. Didn't mean to dump all my neuroses in your lap on a first date." There's an embarrassment there that's sweet and compelling.

"Don't apologize. I think it's fascinating. So many layers to you, Beth Lamont."

Her eyes sparkle now. "What about you? Where do you fit?"

I shrug. "I thought I fit in the army pretty good but that changed when I came home. I guess I haven't been here long enough to say if this place fits or not. If the discussion in class today is any indication, it's going to be challenging, to say the least."

"Why?"

"Because these are useless thought experiments. It doesn't teach you how to make these decisions in real life. When no matter what you decide, someone is going to die." Her green eyes are intense. Curious. She's unflinchingly honest when most people avoid any real talk about the war. Most folks say we support the troops until those troops bring up what really happens in war. Then they quietly change the subject. But not Beth.

"I don't spend a lot of time thinking about what you guys do during war. I spend most of my time pissed off at how we take care of people like my dad when they come home."

Her hand is tense now, beneath mine. We're treading into dark waters. Moving beyond a conversation about thought experiments and business school ethics into something dangerous and personal.

"I think they're tied together," I say.

"You're probably right." She finally slides her hand free to take a drink. "But it's not my place to judge. My dad came home. I'm not going to question what he did in order to make that happen."

"I'm not sure our classmates would be so forgiving," I say.

"Just wait. At least you're not in any political science classes where you'd hear about the American hegemony and racist imperialism."

I laugh because she sounds so disgruntled. "Not a card-carrying hippie?"

"Not exactly."

She's relaxed again as the waiter brings our food. She keeps glancing at her watch every few minutes. I'm curious enough to finally ask if she's going to be late for an appointment.

I am not prepared for her response.

Chapter Nine

Beth

"I have to take my dad to the hospital."

There's no point in lying to him. He's caught me staring at my watch. I could make something up about a nervous habit but I'm not that quick on my feet.

"His back?"

"He's out of pain medication," I tell him. God but the honesty hurts. It sucks. "The only way to get him through until his appointment is to take him to the ER."

I can't bring myself to be totally honest though. To tell him about my father's dance with alcohol and pain medication and everything in between that keeps him in the constant limbo. It feels like he'll never escape.

And I won't either.

But Noah catches my sleight of hand. "Why do you have to wait to take him?"

I want to avoid the answer. The hard truth of my life. I don't want to tell him about Dad having to sober up before the ER can treat him, or the lies I've told to get him medication when he needs it, or the alcohol I've bought with my fake ID.

I stab a piece of chicken, trying to come up with anything other than the truth.

"It's easier if we go after I'm out of class for the day." A weak story. I can practically feel the weight of my lie on my tongue. It's like a blazing neon sign over my head.

Noah's eyes tell me he's not buying it. There's a skepticism in those dark brown depths. I'm not ready to share all the dirty little details of how I'm making it through school taking care of my dad. Trust is a fragile thing. Something I don't give away easily.

More than anything, I don't want his pity. I don't want to answer the questions about why don't I leave him to take care of himself. Why am I working so hard when my dad isn't? Or the accusations that I'm being held back by my dad.

I won't hear it again.

My heart aches a little as I brace for the inevitable. My chicken is deeply interesting at the moment. I want to change the subject, but my words are locked in my throat.

But Noah continues to surprise me.

"You're amazing, you know that?"

I freeze. His answer is completely unexpected. There is sincerity in his brown eyes. Something close to respect. It's not an emotion I'm used to seeing looking back at me. I don't know what to say.

It's hard to breathe all of a sudden. I want badly to go back to the parking garage. To take things back to simple, like they were before. When he kissed me and there was nothing else between us.

But now he's told me that I'm amazing, and it doesn't jive with anything in my brain.

"That's a nice thing to say." Great, now I'm arguing with him over a compliment.

He sets his fork down and folds his arms on the edge of the table. I can suddenly see Noah the soldier watching me and it is not a comfortable feeling. I imagine his soldiers felt two inches tall when they were subject to this look. My dad used to have the same look when I messed up when I was little.

He hasn't given me the look in a long time.

But Noah watching me now is disconcerting at best. I don't know what to say.

"I was on guard duty once with this lieutenant. He'd gotten married before he left, but his wife got sick. Thyroid cancer. I remember because he was talking about how easily it was cured. Like, if you've got to get cancer, get this one." He pauses, takes a drink of water. "He tells me he's filed for divorce. When I ask why, he tells me it's because he wants to have kids. If she's already gotten sick at twenty-three, he's not going to be saddled with her and her health problems his whole life. Time to cut sling load and all that."

Revulsion squeezes my throat. "He sounds like a pretty horrible person."

Noah nods, sipping his water. It's a long moment before he speaks again. "I think so. He was cheating on her with the supply clerk, too."

"Sounds like a real charmer." I want badly to turn the conversation to something less depressing than cancer and infidelity.

"He was a shitbag, but it surprised me how many people I talked to afterward who agreed with him. Like they were completely mercenary about taking care of family. They wouldn't risk what they've worked so hard for." He takes a drink. "I think you can be like that until you've been through some bad stuff," he says after a moment. "Then you kind of hope you've found someone you can count on, you know?"

"My mom left us," I tell him. Because why not just put my entire life story out there, right up front, so he knows what he's dealing with. "When Dad got hurt. The first time he was laid up for more than a week, she shacked up with his platoon sergeant. Filed for divorce and took off." He's listening, no judgment in those sexy dark eyes.

I don't know why I'm telling him this. We're not a thing. He's going to a top twenty school; he's doing well enough in life. He hasn't been taking care of a hurt dad since he was sixteen. He doesn't need to know what my life entails. And yet, I tell him. Not everything. But a lot. A lot more than I tell most people.

And he listens. Really listens.

He pays the bill and holds the door once again. We walk toward his car, his shoulder bumping against mine. After a moment, I feel his fingers sliding down the top of my hand until his fingers thread with mine.

I hold on tight. Because I'm afraid that this might all be a dream that comes crashing to a halt just when things start to get good.

Noah

I wasn't lying when I told her I thought she was amazing. My words clearly make her uncomfortable. I can't help reaching out to her. To make sure she is real. People like her are so rare in this life.

As we walk to my car, I pause near her door. Anticipation curls through my belly. Her fingers tighten in mine as I lean in closer, cupping her neck with my free hand. "Thanks for letting me buy you lunch," I whisper against her mouth.

She makes a warm sound deep in her throat. The sound vibrates beneath my fingertips. I brush my thumb over her pulse, and it scatters under my touch. I want to feel her tremble. I want to pull her close and feel her body against mine, skin to skin, but I'm afraid to rush her. Instead, I nibble on her bottom lip. A gentle tug. She rewards me with a gasp, a quick rush of breath against my skin.

Then she slips her fingers free of mine and slides her arms around my neck. She threads them through my hair, her nails scraping against my scalp. "I enjoyed it very much," she whispers, a moment before she opens completely for me.

Her tongue slides against mine, questioning, tasting. My hands slide down her back, pressing her closer to me. Her back is strong and slim. I love the feel of her soft strength against me. I want to be alone with her. To explore her body, the hard and soft contours. To discover where she likes to be touched. I want to feel her fingers on my skin.

I still then, ceasing my exploration. That would mean showing her my scars.

I'm not ashamed of them. I long ago made peace with how they came to be and what they mean for the rest of my life.

But I'm not sure I want to answer those questions yet. My

fingers tighten on her lower back. She moans quietly into my mouth and I forget about the scars on my body and am lost completely in the taste and touch of her. Her nails dig into my skin and all I can feel is her, everywhere.

I'm not a warrior monk. I've been around the block a time or two, but there is nothing like feeling Beth pressed against me, her body swaying in time with mine.

"God but you can kiss," she murmurs.

"I can get used to being called God." Because I can't possibly think of anything cornier to say.

She laughs and it's like warmth and sunshine against my soul. Yeah, maybe I was a little bit of a poet in another life. A bad one but hey.

"Thank you very much for lunch."

"I think I'd like to see about taking you for dessert."

"Sad trombone noise," she says, but she's smiling and everything is right in my world. "I'm really glad I'm not here because of your strength in pick-up lines."

"We all have weaknesses," I say. But I haven't let her go, and her body is still pressed to mine. I want to keep her there, to protect her and shelter her from the reality of whatever she's getting ready to face with her dad.

In truth, I'm not sure I'm in any shape to have anyone in my life, but Beth is too tempting to let my better judgment take hold. Her body against mine makes me feel alive for the first time since I came home from the war. In her arms, I've found a place I fit, that feels *right.*

I slip my hand beneath her prim sweater and run my thumb down the center line of her spine. She shivers, but doesn't pull away. Her nails massage my scalp. I trace the same line over her skin. She makes that warm noise in her throat again. I press my lips to the spot.

"I wish we had more time." She tilts her head to one side in an offering that is so damn sexy, I'm ready to beg her to come back to my place with me.

I've got a sudden blinding fantasy of her naked in front of me, her back arched beneath my touch. I want to run my hands over her smooth skin and soothe the tension from her muscles until she turns to liquid in my arms.

"But duty calls."

She smiles, but it doesn't reach her eyes. "Thank you for understanding."

I cup her face then because she sounds so sad it almost breaks me. "I admire you for what you're doing. A lot of people wouldn't."

"My dad gave up everything for me to be here in this program," she says. "I won't walk away from him just because things get tough."

I can't help but wonder what *everything* means, but I don't push her on it. I suddenly want her to trust me enough to tell me about it. I'm curious about her dad. About a man who could raise a daughter as steadfast and loyal as Beth is.

I kiss her then because I'm falling. Hard. And there will be no soft landing for me at the end of this.

Chapter Ten

Beth

He leaves me at the same address as before. I'm not ready to show him the full reality of my life. Maybe that makes me a coward, but I'm enjoying the fantasy I'm building around Noah. That maybe he wouldn't let me down. That maybe he could be someone I could trust.

He said he admired me.

I walk quickly to the house I share with my dad.

It's not admirable to take care of someone you love. It's just what family does. My dad went to war to take care of me. He sacrificed his health so that I could go to college. Taking care of him when he's hurting is a small thing, considering the gifts he's given me.

The TV is off when I enter the house, but I hear the music from his bedroom.

It's never good when the music is playing. It means he's remembering. Maybe good times, maybe bad, but I never know what to do when he's facing the memories.

He's sitting in the old leather chair in the corner of his bedroom. He's showered and sober.

He smiles sadly when he sees me. His face is worn and lined, but he's still the most handsome man I know. His dark hair is greying at the temples, and he's not as big as I remember him from when I was little. But right now, when he smiles and he's all there, I smile back because, in that moment, I've got my dad back.

I know it won't last. The pain meds will take him away

again soon enough, and I know that as soon as he tries to stand, the pain will tear at him all over again.

But I'll still have that moment when he's relatively sober and he hasn't moved yet so the pain isn't overwhelming him.

"You're up."

"Mostly," he says. "How's school?"

"Really good." Because it is. I enjoy school so much more than I did in high school. I truly love my classes. "You doing okay?"

He shrugs. "Well, I got my pants on by myself so that's always a plus." He looks a little sheepish like he always does. I've had to put his pants on him before. "I could use some help with my shoes though."

"Sure thing."

I find his boots near the edge of the bed where I'd put them the last time I took them off. Kneeling down in front of him, I pull his socks on first, then slip his feet, one after the other, into his boots. I double knot them because I know if they come untied, he gets annoyed. Plus, any sudden movements caused by stepping on an untied lace could cause him to black out from the pain.

We're going to take the car. I don't drive it often because well, gas costs money we don't have. And, well, there's parking at the hospital. Add in that the idea of putting him on public transport to the ER involves too much pain and uncertainty and it's just easier to drive him. When it's just me, I tend to take the bus.

His mouth is pressed into a tight, flat line. I know he's hurting and I hate it. I hate the VA for being incompetent in treating him. I hate whoever said his injuries weren't service related. Just a few more percentage points on his disability and things might have been dramatically different.

I stand and offer him my hands. "Ready?"

He takes a deep breath. "Not really."

"Can I get you anything first?"

"This is one of those times where I wish I could find something funny to say. The reality is that I just don't want to move." There's resignation in his voice. We've done this drill one too many times.

He's got to psych himself up to face the pain. Anyone who ever says back pain is just people making shit up has never seen what it does to someone. And the people who do fake it deserve a special place in hell because they take appointments from people like my dad, who need them.

He's not faking. God but I wish he was. There have been too many times, though, when he's tried to pretend he's not hurting.

It's not a good thing to see your father on his hands and knees in the kitchen because he can't get to his feet. It's terrifying when you're sixteen years old and you don't know what to do.

I learned, though. Just like I learned that right now, I need to let him find the courage to stand up. I can't rush this.

All I can do is stand there and wait for my dad to take my hands.

Then I'll lean back and help pull him to his feet. I'll slide beneath his arm and help hold him upright while the pain passes.

Then we'll shuffle out to the car. He'll slowly lower himself into the passenger seat, and I'll help him swing his legs inside. I'll drive carefully to the ER where they'll check us in.

And then the real anger management will start. Because they'll pull up the bills we haven't paid. And ask about insurance that he doesn't have. And I'll be frustrated and angry because all they'll do is get him stabilized. They won't treat him because they're not required to.

But all of that comes after.

First, my dad has to take my hands.

Noah

Part of me wants to go with her to the hospital.

But I hate hospitals more than I hate snakes and spiders

and being caught in small dark places.

Even if I went with her, I'd be next to useless. I'd have to double up on the anxiety meds just to walk through the door and that's not counting what I'd have to do to stay there for longer than a few minutes. Yeah, me and hospitals have some issues.

It's not like hospitals don't send me Christmas cards or anything like that. It's just that I really hate hospitals.

I need to get my homework done and prepare for our tutoring session tomorrow. I know Beth's not going to look at me like I'm some kind of Neanderthal mouth breather, but I still don't want to be a complete imbecile in front of her.

I've got some pride, after all. Just a little bit. You tend to lose a lot when you spend any quality time in a hospital. Tubes and nurses and needles do a number on any dignity you've got left. Who needs self-respect, anyway?

I love the silence of my place. I take my medication, the one that will wind me down but not too much. It's not time for sleep yet. Then I settle into my homework.

Except that my phone vibrates on the table next to me.

Hey we're meeting up at The Pint.

I frown. *We?*

Me, Caleb and Nathan. Nathan is celebrating or some shit.

What's he celebrating?

No clue. Quit bitching and just meet us there.

I have homework. I need to get it done, but I figure I can meet the guys for burgers and beer. Well, maybe not beer. Not really willing to go down the fun little wormhole of beer and anti-anxiety medication. I did that a couple of times. And the few memories I have involve police.

Too many people have pulled too many strings for me to be here for me to screw it up. I text Josh that I'll be there in a bit and get one of my assignments done. I crack open the stats homework, but my eyes cross at confidence intervals.

Beth will help make that clear tomorrow. I finish my reflection essay for ethics. I'll reread it later to make sure it's at least marginally coherent. Then I grab my keys and head into the downtown area where the old tobacco mills have been repurposed into luxury apartments and a foodie paradise. Gentrification at its finest.

I'm not so unaware of the history of the area not to notice the clear lines of demarcation between the problem areas of town and the newly upscale areas. You don't have to be a local to see it. It's stark and there are few areas that serve as bridging areas. Streets are either well off or poor.

The Pint is a microbrewery and there is so much hipster essence vibrating off the walls, I'm sure the guys have picked the wrong place. It's a far cry from Scruffy Murphy's on Broadway where I used to mix it up with guys in the Ranger Training Brigade. The Pint stays open all night, transitioning from a bar to a diner in the early morning. It's a strange mixture of businesses, but it works.

"Slim pickings on bars?" I ask, slapping Josh on the shoulder.

"Wait 'til you have the summer ale before you complain," he says.

I get a beer and pull up a chair to the table. Nachos and potato skins appear magically from the kitchen. Josh is right. The summer ale is awesome.

"What's the occasion?"

Nathan raises a beer. "To lost friends."

Ah, shit. This isn't a celebration. I feel like stabbing Josh for not warning me about this. I don't want to commiserate over people I don't know. I've got enough of my own bad memories.

Caleb raises his glass and I do the same. Solidarity and all that. You never leave a buddy alone when nights like this happen. I wish I didn't understand that. Caleb and Nathan had been deployed together, apparently. "Big firefight outside of Ramadi when we were not fighting in Anbar." Caleb makes air quotes around "not fighting." "Nathan always takes the anniversary hard. Figured I'd get you two sticks in the mud out to help me run herd on him tonight."

Nathan is already well in the bag. The fact that Caleb is

looking out for him tonight makes me respect Caleb, at least a little bit.

Nathan leans in a little closer. "You know what pisses me off?" He's slurring. "The fact that all these fucking pussies in this goddamned place have no idea what we've sacrificed for them."

A big guy sporting a thick black beard and trademark hipster glasses looks over at the pussies comment. Both arms are covered in full-sleeve tattoos. And they're big arms. A hipster who likes the gym, apparently. Ah hell. Scruffy Murph's it isn't, but clearly, Nathan running his mouth isn't going to go unobserved. I hold up a hand to Glasses. "He's having a bad night."

"Clearly." And Glasses is German. Excellent. Never met a German who didn't appreciate a good bar fight, but I'm hoping that maybe hipster Germans are different from the guys who hang out in the fest tents at Oktoberfest.

Hopefully, it won't come to that.

But Nathan is not going to simply drown the memories. And as he gets down and dirty with his, some of my own decide to come out and play.

Jack Johnson's "Flake" comes on. My throat closes off, and I take a sip of the beer. It's impossible to swallow. I can smell the fucking sand again. It got into all the nooks and crannies but right now, I can feel it burning into my cheek again as I lay face down on the ground. The rocket fire keeps coming and through it all, "Flake" keeps playing on my iPod as I pray that I won't die beneath a pile of concrete and debris in this shithole country.

I knock back another pull from the beer. Not a pleasant memory, that's for damn sure. But not much else I can do beyond ride the wave until it decides to leave me alone. Until next time. Or the time after that.

Because it's a funny thing about going to war. It never leaves you alone for long. It's always there. Lurking. Waiting. Skulking in the dark.

And as I sit here with Nathan and Caleb and Josh, it dawns

on me why I feel comfortable with them in a way that I haven't felt around most of my classmates.

They've been there. They get it.

I take another pull off my beer and wonder how things are going for Beth at the hospital with her dad. I wonder if her dad has nights like this where the memories come out and play and all you can do is sit back and hope they'll eventually leave you alone again.

I want to text her. To see how she's doing.

But I don't. Because I'm off kilter enough to know that I shouldn't be around people tonight, and Beth doesn't need to put up with my shit.

I'll take a cab home later. My homework will have to wait.

Because it looks like I'm crawling into the bottle with Nathan and Caleb and Josh.

Chapter Eleven

Beth

I'm trying not to cry. I'm so angry I could scream, but there is little that moves an already unsympathetic nurse like calling her names for something that is completely not her fault.

"We can inject his back, but we can't give him any more of his current pain medication," she tells me.

"He doesn't have an appointment for another week. What is he supposed to do?" My voice is level, and I'm proud of myself. It's a small victory in a losing fight.

"I can give him prednisone. It's a steroid that will help with the swelling. And I can do some muscle relaxers. But he's triggered our medication system. There's no way for the doc to override it and prescribe him Oxy."

"So he's supposed to just be in pain. What about withdrawals?"

"I'm sorry. I wish there were some other way to deal with this, but there isn't. The new system locks certain patients out, and your dad is one of them. The doctor will talk to you about alternative medications."

My throat locks up and my eyes burn. I do not want to cry in front of this woman. He's going to be hurting for more than a week until his appointment.

Which means he's going to crawl into the bottom of a bottle to manage the pain. I want to climb the walls and scream at the unfairness of it. But I don't because having a tantrum doesn't solve anything. It only gets security called.

In the end, I nod and ask what paperwork I need to fill

out.

A few hours go by before they inject him. A little while after that, he's already moving better. I get his prescriptions, but it's still another hour before we can leave. It's almost midnight. An early night for us, all things considered.

I stop by the pharmacy and deal with the reality that I can't pick up everything the doc has prescribed. I take the prednisone and the Tramadol, leaving the Flexeril until I get paid. I hope. I'm not convinced the Tramadol is a good idea, but the doc staunchly refused to prescribe my dad's normal medication. They're not going to do much good, but the double dose of prednisone has worked a little bit in the past. Maybe it'll hold him over until next week. And hopefully the non-narcotic pain medication they gave him will hold him over and not send him into withdrawal.

He's stiff but able to get out of the car on his own. He leans on me as I help him into the house and into bed.

"You get your homework done?" he asks as I'm untying his boots.

"Most of it. I've still got a little bit to do."

"You should get some sleep. You're too young to work this hard."

I toss one boot on the floor, nudging it beneath the bed so he won't trip over it if he gets up in the middle of the night. "It's only temporary, Dad. Once I get a job and get us insurance, I'll take a break. Maybe a nice vacation to the beach after we get your back fixed."

I pour him a stiff drink and hand it to him. I know the injection won't last. The heating pad beneath his back is more to make me feel like I'm doing something for him than actually helping. But he gets cold at night so the heating pad helps there, too. Maybe someday, I'll be able to afford to turn the heat up.

"Night, sugar bear," he says as I pull the blanket over his hips.

"Night, Daddy." My voice breaks, and I leave before he catches it.

I don't cry in front of my dad. I did once, right after mom

left. I was sixteen and he was sitting at the kitchen table back when he could still do things like that. There had been a bottle of tequila in front of him, and he'd been tossing back shots. I'd cried and asked him when mom was coming home.

He'd offered me a shot. Said she wasn't so I should cry and get it all out of my system. She wasn't worth my tears.

I'd sat with him that night. Yeah, I tried the tequila. I don't know why people drink that stuff. It was terrible. I didn't get much beyond the burn at the tip of my tongue before I turned back to water.

But I never cried in front of him again after that.

It wasn't shame or anything. I just never wanted him to think any less of me. He'd gone to war. He'd done so much in life to make sure I would be able to follow my dream of going to school. If I couldn't handle a little stress in life, what kind of person did that make me?

I swipe at my eyes as I try to finish my ethics assignment. I'm not going to cry about this.

My dad came home. He's alive when I have friends whose dads didn't. I'm not crying over some stupid policy and the mindless drones who enforce it like storm troopers.

Except that I am.

Hot tears spill down my cheeks, and I finally surrender. I cover my face with my hands. A single sob breaks free and I tamp it down. I don't want my dad to hear me in our tiny house.

But my heart aches tonight. Because he's hurting and there isn't anything I can do to fix it. I don't have that job yet that can get us insurance and money to pay for whatever surgery he needs that will fix his back so he won't constantly be in pain.

There has to be some way to fix it. The VA has scheduled appointments for surgeries. Surely that means they can do something, right?

The tears keep coming. I bite my hand to make them stop, but I can't. My chest is tight and tonight, it's all coming out. I find one of our dish towels and cover my mouth. Another sob breaks free and it hurts. It fucking hurts that I can't fix this.

That I might never be able to fix this. That my dad might spend the rest of his life in pain because I haven't been able to figure out the medical system that keeps him in pain. There has to be a better way but right now, I can't see my way out of the hopeless morass of the VA system.

I cover my face with the towel and let the tears come. Because I can't do anything else until they stop.

And I still have homework to do.

Noah

I make it home alive. I'm pretty sure I left the cabbie a good tip. I've got his card in my pocket so I can call him in the morning and he can take me back to wherever I left my truck.

I'm not really drunk. Just kind of fuzzy on several levels. Things feel thick, and I can't quite make my feet work right. But I finally make it through my front door, and I think I get it closed behind me.

Bed. There it is. I crawl into it and lay face down long ways. I suppose I should take my shoes off, but they're at the other end of my body and that seems like a really big distance at the moment. I see my stats book on the chair. I have the sudden urge to know if Beth is awake.

I shouldn't text her. It's late, and she works so damn much. If I text her and she's not awake, I'll be the biggest dick for waking her up. I lower my head to my phone. Damn it I just want to hear her voice.

Memories suck. I want to hear her tell me about her dad and chase away the sound of that fucking song that haunts me.

I would have been fine if not for that damn song. And it's stuck in my head now, which makes matters worse.

Don't text her. Don't text her.

My phone vibrates in my hand. I don't dare hope that it's her. That would be more than a little freaking weird.

It's Josh. *Make it home okay?*

That is such a soldier thing to do. Checking on your buddy. It's embarrassing for me to admit how weird it was that there wasn't a phone roster handed out on the first day of class. No one was appointed class leader to make sure that everyone was accounted for. All the students were essentially on their own, and it was a completely foreign idea to me. No one needed to check on anyone else. I wasn't responsible for anyone but myself.

I have to admit that it made me feel a little useless. I made sergeant at twenty, which meant that I spent most of my brief life as an adult watching out for other people. Checking on their barracks rooms, making sure they were where they were supposed to be when they were supposed to be there. Making sure I had everyone accounted for after indirect fire hit our base.

Making sure everyone left was on a flight home when we left country. Counting people had become second nature to me - and now I didn't have to do it anymore. None of us did.

But there's good ol' Josh, checking on me. I was supposed to be the sober one. Not tonight, apparently.

My phone vibrates in my hand again.

Yep. In bed now. My thumbs feel fat and clumsy, and I have to squint to make sure I've typed what I meant to type. LT used to harp on us about the perils of drunk texting. It was part of his weekly safety briefing speech: don't put anything in a text that could be used against you in a court martial.

Sleep tight. Don't let the sand fleas bite.

Not funny.

Sand fleas were definitely not funny. Nasty little fuckers. Amazon.com must have made a small fortune shipping flea collars to us. Man didn't the commander flip out when he caught us wearing flea collars around our boots. He'd said the permethrin treatment should have worked fine. Yeah, well it hadn't, and we were getting tore up.

One of my soldiers had been evac'd back to the states with leishmaniasis, which had left us a man short in the stack for patrols. Things had gone to shit shortly after he'd left, too. Lucky bastard missed out on all of the fun stuff.

I lower my head to my forearms and let myself drift in a

hazy fog. I'm going to pay for this tomorrow. I've never been a big drinker, so when I do drink, I pay for it. I was never one of those guys who could stay out until PT formation, puke on the run and keep going. I a nonfunctioning ball of misery when I'm hung over; there's was no other way to put it.

My phone vibrates in my hand again. A phone call, not a text. I squint but can't read the number so I just hit the green icon.

"Y'allo." Silence. I squint and make out the number. Oh shit, it's Beth. "Hey," I say, hoping that I'm not slurring.

"Were you sleeping?"

"Nope, just lying here." Mostly the truth. I don't think sleep is in my future any time soon tonight. More like drifting on fuzzy clouds until my alarm goes off. "How's your dad?"

Silence again. "Beth?"

"He's okay. They gave us a really hard time about his medication. I feel like it was a waste of a trip."

"Are you all right?"

"I...Not really."

Tomorrow, part of me will be really fucking happy that she called me tonight. Right now, though, another part of me hurts for her. I can hear the pain, the fatigue in her voice. "Is there anything I can do?"

A quiet sigh. "I don't know. I just...I didn't want to sit here alone in the dark."

Fuck fuck fuck. I could go to her if I hadn't been drinking. I don't want to tell her that though. I've let her down. Left her alone.

Maybe there's another way.

"Did I ever tell you about the time we filmed a music video downrange?"

A choked sound that I hope is a laugh. "No I don't think you mentioned it."

"Yeah. You know that 'Call Me Maybe' song?"

"How could I not?"

"We totally did choreography and everything. LT put it up on YouTube but then it went viral and the brigade commander found out about it. He was not amused."

She laughs and some of the tension around my heart eases off a bit. "What happened?"

"Well, LT got a sharply worded ass-chewing while the rest of us got the sergeant major's boot in our collective asses along with extra guard duty."

"I don't suppose this video has been immortalized anywhere? It sounds like something my dad would like."

"You don't want to check out my dancing skills? I was on top of a container in PT shorts and a reflective belt with three other dudes doing a line dance."

She's laughing again and I smile. "I think I like the image of you as business school student. I'm not sure what seeing you dancing would do to my impression of you."

"It's very masculine, I swear." I'm resting my head against my forearm, holding the phone to my ear. It's kind of surreal, lying there in the dark, talking to her as the world spins slowly beneath me.

"Noah?"

"Hmmm?"

"Thanks for making me laugh."

My eyes burn suddenly. Her words make me think she hasn't had a reason to laugh in a long, long time. I know the feeling.

"Any time. I'm full of stories about me dancing in Iraq."

She makes that warm sound that I'm starting to love. "Good night, Noah," she whispers.

"Good night, Beth."

The silence is back, but now, it's a good silence. The song is gone from my head, replaced with a happier memory of that fucked up deployment and the comforting thought that Beth called me tonight when she needed someone.

That alone is worth the price I will pay for the hangover tomorrow.

Chapter Twelve

Beth

The sun is already up when I finally slide out of bed. It was a long night. I'm not sure why I called Noah last night, but I'm glad I did. I try to picture him dancing on top of a shipping container and can't quite create the image but it makes me smile.

I slip a sweatshirt on over my tank top and head into the kitchen.

I stop in the doorway. "Dad?"

He's upright, standing over the stove, cooking something that smells like a mixture of heaven and awesome. Because it is really hard to screw up just-add-water pancake mix out of a box. And I'm not entirely sure the mix isn't expired but I'm not about to say something and ruin the morning.

He waves a spatula in my direction. "I was hoping you'd be in bed a little longer."

"How are you upright?" He could barely move last night and now he's cooking breakfast?

"I have no idea what was in that shot last night but I'm mobile. I thought I'd cook my little girl some breakfast for taking such good care of her old man."

I walk over and put my arms around his waist. He kisses the top of my head and it feels good, so good to have my dad hug me. To have him fully in the room at the moment and not spaced out on pain medication.

I lean my head against his shoulder for a moment, hoping that this isn't a dream. "Last night was kind of rough," I finally say.

"Yeah." He leans his cheek against my head and I want to stay there forever. "Maybe this time, the meds will last a little longer and I'll actually get the surgery."

I pull away then. What I'm about to suggest is basically financial suicide but I can't come up with any other options. "What if we pay for the doctor and the surgery outright?"

He flips the pancake he's managed to mangle in the pan. It's a disaster, but I don't care. I sneak a look at the date on the box. Not expired. Winning all the way around.

"We can't afford that, sugar bear. And we probably don't have the credit, either. Something like that would break us."

We're already broken, but I don't tell him that. I've been handling the bills since Mom left. Dad's been too in and out of things to do it reliably, and after the first couple of times the electricity had been shut off while I was still in high school, I took over.

I don't tell him about the stack of unpaid bills in the box near the kitchen table. It doesn't do any good to make him worry about them.

I'll graduate in another year. Hopefully, get a job. Grad school was a possible option, but I'm pretty sure it's a long shot. A job is a better choice. Hopefully one that will enable us to pay down some of the debt. That will keep him from running out of medication.

"I don't like seeing you hurting like this, Dad."

"I know. Trust me, I don't like you seeing me like this, either. No parent wants their kid to have to take care of them." He slides the disaster of a pancake to a plate then starts another one. We don't have much by way of food, but we try to make what we've got last. Eggs, potatoes. There are about a dozen different ways to prepare them so that you get multiple days of food out of them.

You only get sick of certain foods when you have options. Most of the time, though, we don't run out of food. We have to be careful, though.

I've got to meet Noah for our tutoring appointment in a

few hours. That'll be money I can use to pick up the rest of Dad's medicine on my way home from campus today.

"What are you going to do today?" I ask.

"See if the guys at the shop need any help."

When he's able, my dad works part-time for a computer repair shop near campus. It's an under-the-table job because he's not reliable enough to be there full-time, and he doesn't want to take a payroll slot away from someone who can.

He likes fixing things. Our kitchen table is a score he'd rescued from a yard sale several years ago. Before he'd gotten hurt, he'd stripped it down, patched it and refinished it. It is still in our kitchen, a little more worn than when I'd been little.

It's a reminder of what life had been before my dad went to war because he'd transferred his G.I. Bill to me and had incurred a service obligation. What life would be like again, once I figured out how to get his back fixed.

Breakfast is one of the few things he cooks and does well. The mangled and slightly burned pancakes are extra special today because it's been so long since he's been able to get up. I take my time, not wanting the morning to end.

Afraid that when I come home tonight, I'll see him once again on his back on the couch, unable to move because of the blinding pain.

I clean up after we eat, washing the dishes by hand and setting them to dry in the rack. It's an easy thing, spending time with my dad. We talk about nothing in particular.

I want to tell him about Noah, but I'm not sure how to broach the subject. Or what to even tell him. We aren't a thing. Yet. I don't think. Maybe we are.

Maybe some other time. Right now, Dad asks about my classes and I tell him I've got a job tutoring.

"Are you still working at the Baywater?"

"Yeah."

"That's a lot on you, honey."

I shrug. "It's okay. I've got an easy class load this semester." Which is only partially true. Writing papers is easy for me, and my two main classes require weekly reaction assignments and an end of term assignment. No exams, which is nice. I'm TAing Stats for Professor Blake and earning credit in my minor.

It isn't terrible. And besides, I think I'm going to enjoy tutoring Noah a lot more than I thought I was going to.

My perceptions of him as a former soldier were completely off base. Now, though, I don't know how to get back on normal footing with him.

Maybe we established a new normal last night. It was certainly going to be interesting. I get ready and kiss my dad good-bye. Hoping that the medication will last more than a few hours. Because it was nice, really nice, having my dad back, even if it was only for a little bit.

It is a reminder of why I am working so hard.

Because I want my dad back.

Noah

I'm nervous and the anxiety medication isn't doing its trick today. I double up an hour before I'm supposed to meet Beth, after picking up my truck before it kicks in, so I'm not driving while fuzzy. It doesn't get me high but sometimes, my reaction to a double dose isn't what I expect. I find a parking spot off campus on the side of the road near some luxury apartments. I suppose if you've got the money to pay for school at this place, you can put your kid up in a nice place, too.

Not the kind of problems I ever expected to have. I'm not broke, but I damn sure don't have two grand a month sitting around for a place like that. Besides, I'm not sure I'd want to live this close to other people.

I shoulder my bag and head out at a good clip toward campus. I'm not far from the business school but it's about a twenty-minute walk to the library where I'm supposed to meet Beth.

I want to know how she's doing after last night.

I'm dying to see her again.

I woke up this morning, my body tight and tense. I'd

drifted into that space between sleeping and waking, and damn if I hadn't imagined pulling Beth into bed with me. I wanted her hands on my body, her head on my shoulder. I wanted to feel her beneath me. Her breath on my skin.

Hell, I'm already reacting to the idea of seeing her again. I need to get my head straight before she thinks I'm some kind of walking erection.

I keep circling around the thought that she called me last night. It was a call that had nothing to do with sex and everything to do with something else. Something a hell of a lot more powerful than a quick screw.

I pass beneath a bridge. In the shadows, I see a couple pressed together in the darkness. An erotic, hidden embrace. My brain detours to thinking about Beth like that. Open in my arms in a stolen moment. Letting my hands caress her skin.

I rub my hand over my mouth. It's a good thing I've got the walk to try and pull my thoughts together. I can't get the couple out of my mind, though. They're burned into my memory. His hand had been just there at the front of her pants, his thumb caressing her hipbone. There had been an eagerness in the way she'd arched into his touch.

Would Beth let me touch her like that? Would she make that little sound in her throat that I loved if I kissed her neck? Christ, I'm a disaster. At this rate, the walk to the library was getting me more wound up, not less.

I stuff my hands into my pockets, wishing the medication would kick in to distract me from the aching need that is growing harder to ignore. It's been too long since I've gone out and gotten a little bit wild. I stopped hooking up when my phone started ringing in the middle of the night with my troops' problems. I mean, I'm not a saint by any stretch of the imagination but it's been a while for me, to say the least. I need to build up my stamina up before I see about taking Beth Lamont someplace alone. There is something about Beth that makes me want to make sure I do things right, and being quick on the trigger isn't going to leave a good impression.

Just tasting her made me want more than I've allowed

myself to want since I've come home. I've been going through the motions since I started school. I am here because other people want me to be here, not because I think I belong.

LT helped get me here. I owe it to him to finish and I will. I met Josh and Caleb and Nathan because he would have wanted me to, and I am glad I did. They are people who speak my language. I don't know where else I might have wanted to be, but I am here now for whatever reason.

And that reason is starting to feel like Beth.

I pause at a crosswalk and sway on my feet a little bit as the meds slam into me. Finally, the blurry, familiar feeling is back. The nervous knot in my belly loosens, and my thoughts stop racing around the hamster wheel in my head like I am on some kind of crazy hyper loop.

Things slow down, and it feels like they are back to normal.

Back to Beth.

A slow smile spreads across my lips as I walk into the library. She's waiting for me near the circulation desk. She's wearing a simple black sweater and slim pants that make her legs go on for miles. Her hair is pinned at the base of her neck, and her small hoop earrings are guaranteed to drive me wild through the entire session.

Her lips part a little when she sees me. I hope that's a good thing.

"Hi," I say. And how's that for eloquent and charming?

"Hey."

"How's your dad?"

"He's good." Her voice is throaty and low. I want to take her someplace private. I'm not sure I can be alone with her in a public space.

I want to run my hands down her thighs.

Fuck, how am I supposed to concentrate on statistics?

"I reserved a carrel for us to use."

"What's a carrel?"

"Study room. I figure we could use it as a place to keep your books and such, now that you're walking to campus."

My mouth is suddenly dry. "Is this like a private space?"

Her eyes darken a little, and she offers a slight nod. I'm speechless. And more than a little aroused.

Chapter Thirteen

Beth

I want this. I don't know how to say the words, so I hope in some weird way that Noah is a mind reader. I tell him about the carrel, and the way his eyes darken makes my skin tighten and burn. He understands what I've done.

The permission I've extended between us.

My body is warm as I lead him up the stairs to the second floor. I can feel his gaze on my back and hips as he follows me. I'm aching as I turn down the hallway that leads to the small room.

It's private, in that there are four walls and a door. The walls are paper thin. The policy says we have to use headphones if we're going to watch any videos.

I doubt we're going to be watching any videos.

And I don't have the slightest idea how we're going to get through his lesson today with the heat burning between us.

He was there for me last night. I called out of a stupid moment of weakness, and he made me laugh.

Now, I can't think of the laughter. I can only feel the heat as I key open the door and step inside.

He steps in behind me. He's there, almost at my back. I hear the faint click of the door as it closes. Noah doesn't move. I'm aware of every inch of his body in the almost space behind me. Every nerve ending is alive, crackling with energy. Heat pools between my thighs. I press them together to stop the ache, and the pressure only makes it worse.

"Is this your space?" he asks. His voice is ragged and thick.

His breath is hot against my neck but still he doesn't touch me.

"Yes." I release a shuddering breath. I’m afraid to turn, to see the arousal in his eyes. "It's a policy violation to..."

"To what?" He skims his fingers over my neck, and I bite back a whimper. "To touch you?" He slides his fingers down my scattering pulse. "I've wanted to touch you since I first met you."

I close my eyes and tip my head a little, offering myself to him. He nibbles gently on my ear, his breath teasing my skin. I can't think of anything beyond the feel of his lips on my skin. Need is hammering wildly between my thighs. Never in my life have I been so aroused by such a simple touch.

He shifts then, pressing his big body into my back. His hand covers my mouth before my cry escapes. I want, oh God, how I want this. I want him. I grip his forearms, needing something to do with my hands. I'm barely standing at this point. I want to sink to my knees and take him down with me. He's hard and pressing against my back, rocking gently as he continues the assault on my throat. My ear. My soul.

"I want to do this right," he whispers. "I want to lay you down in my bed and strip your clothes off you piece by piece." I arch against him and can feel the hard length of him against the cleft of my ass. He slides one hand down the center seam of my body. Skimming the space between my breasts until his palm is flat against my belly. His hand is big and solid and rough, and I want him lower, lower. I shift, opening for him to touch me there, just there. "I want to feel you come against my mouth."

Lower. Please lower. "Touch me." A harsh demand. A plea.

"Here?" His palm slides against the front of my heat, just above where I need him. I make a sound, spread a little further. Urging him silently to please touch me. "Say yes, Beth." A nip on my ear. "Please say yes."

"Yes."

He slides his hand down now, between my aching thighs. The pressure drives me that much closer to the edge. I'm wet. I can feel it through my thin pants. I know he can feel it. He presses hard against me, the heel of his palm caressing me where I'm swollen and wet for him.

"Can you come for me? If I touch you like this, can you come?"

He's whispering again, dirty things I've only read about. I rock against his hand. I want his skin on mine. I want to be skin to skin, flesh to flesh. I want to feel his heat against me. I want his fingers where I'm wet and aching.

But he simply continues his gentle assault. Winding me up higher and higher until I'm writhing against his hand, needing just a little more. My nails dig into his flesh. He turns my head until he captures my mouth with his and I'm making sounds that are lost on the breath between us.

And then it hits me, crashing over me until I'm nothing but trembling nerves firing over and over against the raw and sensitive flesh that he still has not touched skin to skin.

He's kissing me, bringing me back from the edge that I've tumbled over. Soft, petting caresses now. Tempered and tame, slowly bringing me down, back to earth.

I turn in his arms, unsteady against his solid length. I can do nothing more than rest my head against his neck and breathe for a moment, pulling myself back together.

And all the while, he's stroking my back, my hair, my arms. Like I'm the most precious thing in the world to him. I stand there for a moment, lost, forgetting everything but the feel of Noah Warren surrounding me, embracing me.

Holding me upright against the onslaught of sensation he has brought to life.

Noah

I'm destroyed by her reaction. I knew holding her would be too much, too powerful, but I had no idea how unrestrained, how wild she would be in my arms.

I was right to keep us both dressed. There is no way to do what I want with her. Not here when anyone can walk by the door and see in the tiny window.

She's trembling in my arms. I want badly to take her home with me. To bring her to my quiet place.

Slowly. I need to go slowly with her. Not just for her sake, but for mine, too.

This is new territory for me since I've been home. And Beth...Beth is worth the wait.

I lean back, cradling her face. Her cheeks are flushed, her lips swollen from mine. "God, but you're fucking beautiful."

"You're not so bad yourself." Her voice is like liquid honey, thick and rich with arousal. She brushes her lips against mine. "We really should get started on stats. I have to be to work in two hours."

The thought of her in that fitted white button-down shirt does something to my insides. I clear my throat and reach between us to adjust my pants. Her hand covers mine, sliding over the back of my palm. It's an erotic embrace, something unexpected and sensual. She presses her hand against mine and the pressure against my erection is intense. I shift then, sliding her hand beneath mine so that she's cupping my cock. I'm so hard it hurts.

"Seems like that's going to be a distraction," she whispers.

My brain goes completely off the rails as I imagine her dropping to her knees in front of me. I squeeze her hand around my cock, trying to remember that once upon a time, I had more control than a horny teenager. That I had discipline and motivation and, holy hell, her hand sliding over my erection is driving me quietly insane.

"Can I pick you up when your shift is over?" Now is probably a terrible time for a blowjob joke. I can't summon the willpower to take her hand away. The gentle friction isn't enough. It's everything, the center of my whole world. I want more.

"I'd like that." A promise in those words, a promise that I cannot wait to unwrap slowly, so slowly.

She slips her hand up my belly and I immediately miss the warmth of her touch. "So. Stats?"

I nod, my mouth dry, my erection painful. I have no clue how I'm supposed to think about anything other than her naked and writhing in my arms, but there are probably worse problems to have.

She sits in one chair; I take the other. Our thighs are touching and we are shoulder to shoulder as we lean over my textbook.

She explains confidence intervals in a way that actually penetrates the sexual haze in my brain and makes sense. I do a couple of problems by hand, and she checks my work. I like having her watch me. Knowing that she's making sure I'm getting it right.

Sitting here and scratching out equations, I focus on the mental energy required to make sense of it. The reward is the gentle press of her thigh against mine. Not erotic at the moment. Comforting. Steadying.

Holding me upright when I could fall away amid the fear of failing, falling flat on my face. I'm working now, and the problems are clicking in a way they've never clicked before. Like the language is suddenly making sense.

She corrects me when I make a mistake, the tapered point of her fingertip gliding over my chicken scratch writing. I glance over at her. She's focused and serious Beth now. She meets my gaze, and her cheeks flush.

"I love seeing you blush." The truth, I decide, is probably the best track with her. Her flush deepens. "It's true. You've got this amazingly pale skin that turns this gorgeous pink." I lean closer because I cannot help myself. "I want to see how far down your body it goes."

She offers a throaty laugh then taps the paper. "Focus." But she's smiling, the first time I've really seen her smile since I've met her.

I do as she asks, and I work through the other problems she's assigned as extra work. I'm motivated now, not just to get them done and get them correct, but to get through them so maybe I can steal a few more moments of her time before she has to leave.

There are so many things competing for her. Her dad. Her work. School. I'm selfish enough to want my own time, my own space. More than a few hours a week of tutoring.

She's not there yet. Patience. I need a plan. I need to find a way to become part of the space in her life.

Because she is more than fire in my arms.

She's life. And I crave her more than breathing.

Chapter Fourteen

Beth

We actually managed to do his work. I'm kind of amazed that we accomplished anything but somehow it happened. I head to the pharmacy and pick up my dad's prescriptions with the money Noah pays me.

I don't let Noah drive me. He wants to, but his car is in the other direction off campus and I'm already halfway to work with the detour by the pharmacy. I promise to wait for him at the end of my shift. I'm not closing tonight, which means I'll be done by ten.

I call dad and check on him. He's short on words. It happens when he's neck deep in a project. My heart does a little flip that he's working. He'll be distracted for however long it takes him to fix the computer.

Which means that for once, I can steal a few minutes for myself and not worry that I need to rush home.

The good days - when he has them - are really, really good.

My heart is a little lighter. I had enough money for dad's medication. Even though it's not what he usually takes, I'm hopeful that with the injection, it might just keep the edge off the pain until his next appointment that, please God, won't be canceled.

I sail through my shift. Abby comes in and catches me smiling to myself.

"So what's his name?"

Part of me feels guilty that I'm so transparent. On the other hand, maybe I am a crappy friend for not sharing that there was something interesting happening in my life. She knows a little bit about my dad, but I don't tell her too much. I'm not ashamed, exactly, but I hate, hate the pity that usually accompanies people knowing.

Abby is one of my closest friends. The one I call in emergencies and who makes me laugh no matter what. She's gorgeous, with skin the color of rich coffee and beautiful natural curls. I'm jealous of her flawless complexion. She tells me she's jealous of the fact that I can go to the drug store for makeup and not have to spend a fortune on color-matched foundation.

We've been friends since we both started at the Baywater, and she adopted me. Yeah, I have to work through school but she's taught me how to blend in, even at work.

I flush a little bit, and even in the dimly lit hallway near the drinks, she catches me. "Oh, this is news." She leans in closer with a conspiratorial whisper. "Spill. Seriously. I haven't seen you this hot and bothered...ever, now that I think about it."

"Noah. A guy I'm tutoring in stats."

She shoots me her "yeah, right" expression. "Is 'stats' a euphemism for penis?"

I cover my laugh before our boss hears me and comes to investigate. "Well, it wasn't when it started but things have gotten a little...interesting." I breathe out. "He's picking me up after work."

Abby's eyes light up. "You have protection, right? You're not going to lose your damn mind and do something stupid?"

I pause because, no, I don't have any condoms. I'm on the pill for several reasons but still...

"Gotcha covered." She tugs me into the break room and pulls a discreet bag out of her purse.

"You carry these around?"

"Let's just say they're a holdover from my last relationship."

I frown at her. "Abby, you haven't been with Robert in six months."

She rolls her eyes. "It's not like they're expired. Sheesh. I just never got around to taking them out of my purse." She presses the small cloth bag into my hand. "Put them to good use."

I shake my head but slide them into my bag. Because she's right. We've both been careful since we got to school. Girls like us don't have the means to raise a baby and finish school. Babies are the end of any aspirations we might have for a better life through education.

She's watching me, waiting for me to answer the questions she has not asked.

"This is kind of serious for you, isn't it?" There's a sense of wonder in her voice.

"I don't know." An honest answer if nothing else.

She says nothing for a moment at the uncertainty in my voice. "I don't think I've ever seen you not sure about anything. So I think that means this is important." She brushes my hair off my shoulder. "He better be worth it."

There's a reason why I love Abby. I lower my head to her shoulder for a moment, letting myself absorb her strength and confidence. She's amazing in so many ways. I love her for watching out for me. It's nice to be worried about, for once, instead of being the one doing the worrying.

"I think he might be," I whisper. "I think we need to get back to work before Dave comes searching for us."

"He'll probably just inspect our shirts for the appropriate amount of tension across our tits."

She's not wrong.

We hit the floor, delivering drinks and food and chatting with clients. I manage not to screw up any orders even though my thoughts are a million miles away, on Noah.

I usually stay on for extra hours, needing the few more measly dollars I can scrape by for tips. But tonight is already a slow night, and if not for Abby distracting me with tales from table twelve, I die of boredom.

And as I'm heading for the door, Noah is there, standing in the foyer of the ridiculously expensive country club. He's wearing the same light blue button-down shirt from earlier.

He's relaxed and more than a little rumpled.

It warms my soul that he's waiting for me.

Abby walks by. "Hey, Noah. Take care of our girl."

I flush as a slow smile crawls across his lips. "You were talking about me?"

"Maybe."

"Hopefully not about how terrible I am at stats."

I choke back a laugh and he lifts one eyebrow. "Abby asked if stats was a euphemism for something else. My mind just took a detour, that's all."

He steps into my space. Close enough that I can smell the soap on his skin. "I wonder if it's the same one mine just took."

I press my lips together as the warmth is back, spreading like a languid heat through my veins. "We'll have to find out, won't we?"

Noah

She's got time. When she tells me that she doesn't have to rush home, all the blood leaves my brain and goes to the not-rational place in my body.

She slides into the car and closes the door. "I, ah." Shit. Every bit of finesse has left me.

And she laughs at me a moment before she cups my cheek and kisses me. A soft, sucking kiss that sends rational thought over the edge and leaves nothing but sensation in its wake. "Can we go to your place for a little bit?"

"At least one of us is thinking clearly."

"I wouldn't go that far. I was distracted my entire shift."

She looks tired and gorgeous all at once.

"How far from campus do you live?"

"Twenty minutes. Small place off a big house around a farm pond."

"How do you afford it?"

"It's cheaper than living in town." I turn down the dark country road, leaving the city behind us.

She leans against the window, peering up at the bright

night sky. "Wow. I forgot how bright the stars can be."

There's a ridiculous pleasure beneath my heart at the wonder in her voice. I don't want to remind her of life back in the city, but I can't help it. I have to do the responsible adult thing.

"Your dad's okay?"

She makes that warm sound in her throat. "Yeah. Whatever they injected him with last night has really made a difference." She sighs quietly. "I love it when he's up and not hurting." She tips her head toward me as I pull into the driveway of my small house. "He's fixing a computer right now. Lost in circuit boards and memory cards."

"He fixes computers?"

"When he can, yeah. He's pretty good at it. He'd almost gotten hired on at one of the local tech companies, but they opted not to because of his back."

I frown. "That doesn't sound right."

She shrugs, and her voice is resigned. "When the company pays your insurance and you've got a potentially expensive preexisting condition, it can absolutely disqualify you from a job."

Her words are like ice water in my veins. I've got a shitload of things that probably qualify as preexisting conditions.

And I am about to show her more than a few of them.

"That's why I'm in business school," she says. "It's my best shot at getting a job that will pay enough that I can pay for his treatment outright."

"I thought insurance couldn't deny people anymore."

She shakes her head then leans forward to peer out at my small house in the headlights of my old truck. Water from the pond reflects in the moonlight. "Wow, you weren't kidding about the farm pond."

"It's quiet out here."

"It's beautiful." There's a sense of wonder in her voice again, and I don't want to talk about insurance anymore.

I have this ridiculous fantasy of lying her down in the moonlight. I follow her out of the car, coming up behind her. I love the way she fits against me. Like her body is made for mine. I wrap my arms around her, pulling her close.

She sighs into my arms, running her hands over my forearms. Her nails scrape my skin in a gentle caress.

"I've been thinking about you like this since earlier in the carrel." My lips are just near her ear. She shivers in my arms, and I'm ready to fucking melt into her. I can't screw this up.

She makes that sound again, that throaty purr deep in her chest, and I give into the temptation. I press my lips to the space where her throat meets her shoulder, that soft pale indent of skin.

Her nails dig into my skin a little harder when I suckle her there. And when she shifts to rock that gorgeous ass of hers against my cock, I'm damn near done right then and there.

"Can I take you inside?" We both know where this will go if we step inside. I want her to be sure. To be one hundred percent.

I'll stop if she changes her mind. I might cry a little. It's a completely un-masculine thing to do, but I might.

I pray that she says yes.

She rubs her hands down my arms. "I'd like that." A throaty whisper filled with promise.

The moon is bright enough, and my house is small enough that I don't need any lights to see where I'm going. I toe the door closed behind us, and then we're alone in my tiny kitchen. I turn her in my arms so I can feel her softness against me. She's curves and strength and poise and beauty all in one amazing package.

My fingers steal beneath that crisp white shirt. I feel her skin prickle beneath my touch. Slowly, I'm guiding her backward toward my bedroom. The house isn't that big. A few steps and we're there. The bed consumes the space, and for once, I'm eternally grateful I sprang for a bigger mattress when I moved here.

She's warm and soft in my arms, letting me set the pace, the tone.

One more step and I leave her there. She's standing in a

moonbeam, bathed in silvery white light.

Her throat moves as she swallows, and I'm entranced by the motion and the shadows. I'm behind her, keeping her body bathed in the light. I'm barely touching her now, skimming my hands over her arms, barely brushing against the warm fabric of her blouse.

She lifts her hands to that first button. I capture them in mine. "Let me?"

A question, not a demand.

I guide her hands to her sides, finally connecting skin to skin. I slide my hands up her arms to that button. I push it through the tiny slit, revealing her pale, pale skin and the perfect curve of her breasts.

I'm tormenting myself with this, but I want to savor every moment of unwrapping her. I want her out of her head when I slide inside her. I want to be out of my own so I can focus completely on her.

Chapter Fifteen

Beth

My breath is locked in my throat as he undoes another button. My breasts are heavy and tight. I crave his touch. I want his hands on me. But he's deliberate and slow as he pushes another button open.

I open my eyes to discover there's a mirror over his dresser. And he's watching me. Heat floods between my thighs at the realization of what he's doing. It's erotic and sexual and pure sensuality all wrapped together.

He tugs the blouse open. I wish I had a bra that was sexy lace and flowers. It's simple cotton, but when he sees it I might as well be wearing the tiniest bikini. He traces his fingers over the edge of one cup. My nipple tightens at the promise of his touch. He tugs at the edge of my bra until it's finally free. The cool kiss of air is a shock from the loss of the warmth of my clothing.

Then he touches me. A gentle stroke of his thumb over my nipple. He's watching my reaction in the mirror, and I'm lost to the sensation, fascinated by watching his touch tease my body to awareness. My nipple tightens to a smaller bud as he strokes it. Again and again - each touch striking liquid heat between my thighs.

I squirm, shifting my legs apart just a little. Just enough to see his gaze drop down to where I want his touch. His hand, his mouth. Anything to relieve the pressure there.

He drags my shirt off my shoulders and my bra follows. I'm exposed and vulnerable now in the bright moonlight, but he hasn't taken his eyes off mine in the mirror. He's warm at my back as he slides his hands up my soft belly to cup the underswell of my breasts. Almost worshipful, he cups them, his thumbs stroking closer to my nipples.

"Noah."

His name is a prayer. He shifts then, his thumbs circling my nipples. Making them stiffen until I'm ready to beg him for more. I part my legs just a little more. An offering.

"Touch me." I can't manage anything more coherent than that.

He slips the hook free of the loop on my pants and slowly - so slowly - the rasp of the zipper exposes me. I don't know what I expect, but he pushes my pants down, down my hips. He kneels in front of me, sliding my feet free of the fabric.

I can't look in the mirror now. Not with him on his knees in front of me, close - so close, to what I want to ask for. I don't have the needy words to say what I want.

His palms are rough on my legs as he drags them up, higher, closer to my aching core. My thighs are wet and he hasn't even touched me there.

I'm watching him now. It's strangely erotic being completely naked in front of him while he's still fully clothed. His touch stops there, just at the seam of my body. He slides his thumb over my swollen clit, the barest touch. My hips jerk at the sensitive caress.

"Christ, you're wet," he whispers. "Can I touch you?" His questions are an erotic sensation all their own. I manage to nod, my body tight and tense with anticipation.

He urges me back until the backs of my thighs collide with his bed. I sink onto his blankets and sheets and I am surrounded by the scent of him. They're cool against the fire raging along my naked back. His hands brush my thighs farther apart and then his thumb is there again. Stroking. Gently petting me where I'm swollen and wet.

Then his mouth is on me. Soft and warm and wet. Suckling me where I'm most sensitive. I almost come off the bed as he torments me with his tongue. He's done nothing more than flick his tongue over me when I completely come apart in a burst of stunningly bright light and brilliant stars.

I'm vaguely aware of a sound like crinkling foil and then he's there, pressing into the swollen folds of my body. Somehow he's naked and we are skin to skin, flesh to flesh. I wrap my arms and legs around him and urge him closer. I want, I need, the fullness of him. Of Noah.

He's filling me, slowly, inch by inch, riding the shuddering waves of my body until he's deep and thick inside me.

I try to press my hands to his back but he threads his fingers with mine, dragging them over my head. And when he moves, I'm completely lost again in a sea of sensation and hyper arousal that takes me beyond consciousness and into a space where he ends and I begin.

He kisses me, and I am drowning in my taste and his, the pleasure of our bodies mingling on our tongues. The distant edge of orgasm comes roaring back, pulsing through my body with a violence that is utterly destructive, dragging me down and carrying him with me.

I'm gone from this plane of existence, carried into a space where there is only Noah. Only me. And together we crash into the void.

Noah

I hold her close when it's over. I don't know if the earth moved for her, but it damn near tilted on its axis for me.

Little shudders vibrate through her every so often. I can't tell if she's dozing, or if the remnants of her climax are still rippling through her.

It's endearing as nothing else is. I want her again. I want to keep her there in the cocoon of my bed and shelter her from the world. But I know she needs to get home.

And just like that, reality is back, for me at least. I'm reluctant to let her go. I'm terrified that this will be just a dream.

A great dream, but one that I will miss when I wake up. I kiss her shoulder gently.

"I should get you home."

She nods. Her hair is cool silk on my damaged shoulder. She hasn't noticed the scars and I'm anxious to get dressed. If we can avoid that conversation today, it would be the perfect ending to a perfect day.

I'm not hiding exactly, but I'm not sure how to have the conversation yet. Not with someone who matters to me.

She slips from my bed into the bathroom. I take that moment to pull a sweatshirt over my head. I'm pulling on pants as she steps back into the room, her body gloriously naked.

"I want to remember you like this forever." She smiles as she steps into her clothing, piece by piece, reversing what I did earlier.

It's more erotic to watch her dress than it was to undress her. And when she's back in that simple white blouse and black pants, my fantasies are already at a fevered pitch, creatively spinning different ways to enjoy her.

I go to her now because it feels strange not to. I cup her face. "This isn't going to get awkward, is it?" I'm suddenly deeply insecure. It's supposed to be the girls that worry about this stuff, but I'm not so issue-free that the thought hasn't occurred to me. What if I read this entire situation wrong? What if this wasn't for her what it was for me?

"Well, we're not doing naked stats if that's what you're asking." Her lips twist into a teasing grin. "But no, it's not going to get awkward." She brushes her lips against mine. I capture her, holding her close, sipping and savoring her lips for another impossibly long moment.

"Will you be on campus tomorrow?"

"We have class, so yes."

"Can I see you?"

Her lips are back in that smile of hers. "Seeing how we're in the same class, I think so."

I pinch her butt for teasing. She yelps and ends up close enough that I can wrap my arms around her again. "I'll see you in ethics, Ms. Lamont."

"I'll see you in ethics, Mr. Warren."

I drive her home, my hands wandering over her thighs, her neck, her body. I can't keep them from wandering.

I kiss her hard when we stop in front of the same address I've left her at each time before. "Think of me tonight?" she whispers.

"I don't know how I wouldn't."

She disappears into the darkness up the steps. I head back to the quiet of my small house.

I can smell her in my space now. On my sheets. Part of her is still with me.

I'm tempted, so tempted not to take the sleeping pill tonight. So tempted to sink into my sheets and try, just once, to sleep with the memory of Beth's touch on my skin, the feel of her body pressed to mine.

But I'm not a fool. I know what happens if I don't sleep with Princess Ambien. The dreams are bad, the nightmares worse.

And I would hate to see Beth - something good and pure and right in my fucking world for once - dragged into my nightmares.

My only escape is my nightly surrender to the sleeping pills. I pretend to sleep a dreamless sleep. I wake up, rinse and repeat, and hope that maybe the next day won't involve so many pills.

But tonight, as the sleeping pill drags me down, I'm surrounded by Beth's scent. I pretend it's her body I'm folded around instead of the pillow. I imagine it's still warm from her skin. I breathe in deeply, inhaling the memory of her touch, the sensation of her hands on my skin, instead of the clawing, burning memories that usually wait for me in the dark.

Chapter Sixteen

Beth

I deliberately sit away from him in ethics class. I see him the moment I walk in. He's in the back against the wall, just like he was on that first day in stats. It feels like a lifetime ago. His eyes darken to deep brown as he watches me cross the classroom away from him. I feel provocative and aroused again. It's going to be hell to pay attention to moral decision-making knowing he's in the back of the class. I wonder if he'll be as distracted as I am.

I take a seat near the front on the opposite edge of the room. I know he can see me, but I'll be forced to pay attention because it would be too obvious if I turn around to ogle him in the crisp white shirt he is wearing today. It's harder now because I know the feeling of his skin against mine, the hard body that can bring so much heat and pleasure with the faintest touch.

The professor comes in and hands out an unexpected quiz on ontologies. I write furiously, grateful for the distraction behind me. It only works for a moment and then I'm finished, listening to the sound of my classmates' pens scratching on their papers.

I sneak a quick glance over my shoulder.

He lifts one brow in that way he does. Heat floods between my thighs again as I remember his mouth on me. Holy hell, I'm going to go up in flames. I shift in my seat again and face the front of the class.

I barely hear the lecture over the blood roaring through my

veins. This is probably a good reason why I shouldn't date. It's hard as hell to pay attention when all the blood that's supposed to be in my brain is turning my body into a raging hormone.

"If I call your name, I need to see you after class," Professor Earl says.

That's unusual. Someone must have been caught cheating again. Sadly, it's an all too common a thing these days. Copying and pasting off the Internet simply isn’t a smart tactic for passing classes, but time and again, people attempt it and invariably get caught.

"Ms. Lamont. Mr. Warren."

I catch Noah's gaze across the room as Professor Earl calls three more names. He is as confused as I am.

I hate being put on the spot. My stomach pitches, and I lift my bag onto my shoulder. I'm almost sick in two minutes flat.

Professor Earl hands me a small envelope of heavy card stock. That's the kind of thing I wouldn't have ever noticed had Abby not pointed out the difference in paper thickness to me. Heavy card stock meant quality. It means money.

"Morgan Banking and Trust wants to hire a paid intern. This is an invitation-only black tie event. I strongly suggest you treat this event as a prospective interview."

Leave it to Professor Earl to drop a bombshell like that in our laps and leave. He isn't exactly Mr. Personality but then again I suppose that's why he's in academia. Academics are known for their neuroses. Another thing I didn't know until Abby enlightened me.

My hands are shaking as I step into the hall. I feel, rather than see, Noah fall into step with me.

"Why don't you seem happy about this?" he asks as we step outside.

It must have started raining while we were in class. I'm in a daze. I barely feel the cool water hitting my skin.

And then it stops.

Noah's holding a large black umbrella. I can't help but smile. "You're always prepared, aren't you?"

I'm aware of everything about him. The white shirt that has

turned slightly transparent from the rain. The smell of his soap. My heartbeat centers in the space between my thighs. I'm aching for him once more. I want to let the world fall away, to ignore the flips my stomach is doing. I want to be wild for once.

"I try." His voice is throaty and warm. Heavy.

I step into his space. I need the contact to convince myself that this is real. That he's standing here in the rain with me. My fingers run over the hard line of his stomach.

"What are you doing?" His throat moves as he swallows hard. I lean in and press my lips to the spot where his pulse beats visibly beneath his skin. I'm vaguely aware that he's lowered the umbrella, shielding us from the rain and the view of passersby.

"Living dangerously," I whisper. "I would very much like to sneak off with you somewhere for a few minutes."

His free arm comes around my waist and I lean into him. Until then, I haven't realized how much I need the human contact. The touch of another body against mine. The feeling of his hand at the small of my back.

"You know this place better than I do."

I smile at the raw need in his voice. My fingers spasm against his chest a little.

"We're not going to get caught by the campus police or anything?" He sounds completely unworried.

"I hope not," I say. "I'm not exactly in tune with the criminal element around here." I run my fingers down the line of his throat. "But I've got an idea."

It's half-baked as ideas go. A place that I remember from freshman year: the basement of the old science building. Dark and silent, it was a place we'd been dared to run through as part of an initiation that the school didn't officially know about or sanction.

But it is the only place I can think of that would be abandoned at this time of day. And I don’t want to wait.

Because I don’t know how long I have before life pulls me back in, away from Noah and the glorious reprieve I have with him. And I am determined to enjoy it for as long as I can.

Noah

She surprises me. Then again, everything about Beth is surprising to me. She leads me away from the business school and toward the science building, a structure that looks like something out of a dark gothic movie like *The Crow*. Stone gargoyles watch us from their perches as she slips us through a side door.

We're in a wide open study area. Couches and chairs and a small coffee kiosk fill the space. It's sparsely populated, but she leads me down behind a small auditorium to an old door with an Exit Only sign above it.

I'm tight with anticipation as I follow her down the narrow staircase and into the dark. My heart slams against my ribs and I remember how much I fucking hate stairs like this. I'm ready to bolt, to flee back into the light and out of the fatal funnel when she turns to me, sliding her body against mine.

Just like that, the panic morphs into a different kind of arousal. One where I'm hot and tight and tense, but it's pleasure running through my veins instead of fear.

She's fumbling with my pants. I hate that I'm wearing a belt in some vague attempt to pass as a respectable member of the business school. There's one exit light penetrating the darkness. It's shadows and sounds and the brush of fabric against skin.

I feel the cool kiss of air against my erection. Only for a moment and then her hand is circling me, squeezing gently. I close my eyes and let her do what she wants with me. I'm her slave. At that moment, I'd do anything she asked me to.

I want to drop to my knees and worship her. I want to turn her around and pin her to the wall. My thoughts are a tumbled erotic mess.

My brain short-circuits a little when she slides down my body.

"Holy shit."

She's on her knees in front of me. Her mouth is there, just

there. She places a teasing kiss on my hip bone. She doesn't notice the scar. Or maybe she does and simply doesn't care. Her hand slips down my length again. I'm enthralled, watching her with the shadows and the light dancing over her face.

My breath locks in my throat. I fall forward, my arms braced on the cold cement to keep myself upright. She's teasing me. Her eyes sparkle in the dim light.

Then it happens. The gentlest kiss against the tip of my cock.

I'm going to die. That's all there is to it. Slowly, so slowly, she takes me into her mouth, sucking me hard enough that I damn near collapse. Light enough to leave me wanting more.

I'm frozen, rooted to the spot as she uses her mouth to drive me over the edge and into a place that is nothing but sensation and pleasure and darkness. I want to move, to thrust into her warm, moist mouth but I don't. I'm terrified of hurting her. Of ending the most blindingly brilliant pleasure I've ever felt.

I'm ready to come. Fuck, I'm right there. I manage to grip her shoulders and pull her upright. I'm tearing at her pants, struggling to get them down over her hips.

My hands are shaking as I try to get the condom on.

She's facing the concrete wall now, her arms over her head, her back arched. A silent, gorgeous offering. I touch her bare, swollen skin. She makes that sound for me as I stroke her where she's soaked for me.

I want to go slow. To draw out the pleasure. But the minute I sink into her, she arches against me. Urging me deeper. Rocking against me and trying to set her own pace.

"Hurry." A breathless command.

I'm lost in her. I reach between her thighs, stroking her. She's so fucking tight and wet and hot. It's a torment to pull out, only to find the sweetest pleasure again as I sink into her. Again. Over and over the pleasure builds.

And then she's shattering around me. Pulsing and squeezing my body, riding my hand with quiet gasps. There are no other sounds between us. The sensual, erotic slide of bodies.

The slick heat melting the air around us. She's coming, and I'm losing my mind as I pump harder, harder.

Until my own release damn near kills me. I'm frozen, pulsing into her, losing a piece of my soul. Surrendering another piece of my heart.

Chapter Seventeen

Beth

He walks me to work. We're both more than a little unsteady after the basement. I'm not sure who is more off kilter. His hands are shaking as he kisses me.

"You okay?" I ask.

He's edgy now, and I'm not sure why. "Yeah." He tries to grin to hide it, but I'm not fooled. I'm pretty good at reading people. "You?"

"Very much so." He brushes his nose against mine. "I'll pick you up after work?"

I squeeze his fingers. I like this new normal we've established. "I'd like that."

"Let me know if I need to beat anybody up for getting too handsy." He tries to make a joke but it falls awkward and flat. I step closer to him. Press near enough that I can feel the heat of his body. "What's wrong?"

He swallows hard. Blinks rapidly a few times. His hand trembles against my waist. "I'll tell you some other time." He brushes his lips against mine. "Promise."

And then he's gone, leaving me with the echo of our pleasure tainted with a new worry.

I didn't think my heart was big enough to make room for another worry. I was wrong.

I don't have time, though, as I meet Abby in the staff room. "We're getting slammed tonight. Some big production by Morgan Banking Company."

I remember the invitation in my bag. "They're hiring an

intern, apparently, but why are they here tonight?" I pull out the card and barely open it before Abby snatches it from me. Her eyes light up.

"Because they can be," she says like it's the most obvious thing in the world. She's not wrong. She hands me back the invitation. "You realize this is a very big deal, right?"

"I can't go."

She's more scandalized than the time I told her I didn't own any makeup beyond Cherry ChapStick.

"Of course you're going. This is invitation only. One of the professors had to put in a word for you to get this. You're going."

"I don't have anything even remotely close to black tie. And I damn sure don't have the money to spring for something in the next three days."

Abby's face lights up even more. She's devious, sometimes, and when she gets like this, it's hazardous to your health to get in her way. "Oh, we can fix all of those things."

"Abby, I love you, but I've seen your closet."

"My closet is filled with stylish, affordable designs that I find on sale. Yours, on the other hand, is a borderline tragedy despite my best efforts. But I'm not talking about raiding my closet. I know someone who can help us out."

"What? You've got three magic mice that are going to turn into coachmen?"

She smiles, and it's positively blinding. I cannot for the life of me understand why she hasn't found someone since she broke up with Robert. She's beautiful, smart, and strong and has a wicked sense of humor.

Maybe guys are intimidated by her. I know I was the first time I met her.

"What do you mean, you know someone?" I ask her again as we pass in the hall.

But she managed to get sucked into work and I didn't have a chance to ask her again how she was going to make me fit to present at the event. We are slammed busy. Which means it will hopefully be a good night for tips. When the alcohol flows at these events, so does the money. I hate being so mercenary about it, but there it is. It's easy to be cavalier about how money doesn't matter, but when your father's ability to walk hinges from one day to the next on whether you make good tips, it's not so simple.

I smile as an older gentleman hands me his empty scotch glass, and I take his order for another. Top shelf, too.

The tab is going to be steep on this one.

Abby leans into me. "That guy whose drink order you just took is the CEO of Morgan Banking. He's the Morgan in the name. Alistair. Very blue blood, if you get me. His family goes back to the first settlement here in the state."

"Nice."

"He's known for being a hard-ass. Pay attention to him tonight and take notes. There will be a quiz at the event on Friday."

It amazes me that Abby can even think that far ahead. I've got no idea how she's going to make me presentable, but hey, if she wants to play fairy godmother again, then who am I to argue? She's never been wrong before.

But now that she's pointed out Alistair, I'm watching more closely. Paying attention to the conversation as I collect glasses and deliver fresh drinks.

"The current interns are a bunch of spoiled brats." This from a shorter man standing to Alistair's right. "I swear if I hear Kiki giggle one more time, I'm going to commit *hari-kari*."

Alistair smiles tolerantly. "She's young, Tim. I think we were young once."

Tim snorts. "Young. Airhead, you mean. She screws up the simplest job. I have to check even her most basic analysis every time she turns one in. She needs to just find her husband and start practicing her homemaking skills. She's not a good fit for the office." Tim zeros in on me. My heart catches in my throat. "Can I help you?"

I clear my throat and play it cool. "I was just waiting to see if I could get you gentlemen anything else."

Tim turns to Alistair. "I bet this waitress is better at

following directives and thinking on her feet than Kiki Millstone."

Alistair looks right at me but doesn't see me. I'm staff. I'm invisible to people like him. He hands me his glass while Tim moves on to another topic of conversation.

Well, that didn't go as planned. I've learned what Tim doesn't like but nothing about Alistair.

Guess I need to practice more skulking.

I hurry back toward the bar. Abby is plating hors d'oeuvres.

She talks fast, dumping information into my lap that I have no idea how I'm going to use. "He's got a granddaughter at Princeton who is majoring in sociology. She's his favorite. His son is disappointed in her. Wanted her to go to law school instead of becoming a bleeding heart liberal hippie. His words, not mine."

I'm amazed listening to her ramble on facts. "Alistair had a heart attack last year and is rumored to be dealing with his mortality. His son is far more cutthroat than he is."

"The son?"

Abby points to a sharp-dressed, dark-haired man in the corner. He's smooth and polished and wears the jacket like a second skin. He's casual without really trying. He belongs here. It practically radiates off every gesture.

"Howard Alistair Morgan the Second. Named after his grandfather." She smiles at me. "Do you not know your local families? How have you worked here for so long and not been paying attention? Hell, there are buildings at this school named after these people."

Clearly, I have a lot of work to do between now and Friday.

But with Abby in my corner, I have a tiny seed of hope that maybe, just maybe, this might be the break I need to be able to take care of my dad.

Noah

I'm sitting in my truck, waiting for her to get off work. Staring at the invitation. Handwritten on cream-colored heavy paper. It reeks of wealth and privilege.

This is not something I want. It is not something I need. I know how I got this invitation. LT. It has to be. Guess he's still watching out for me, whether I want him to or not.

I don't even know how to *spell* "black tie". I suppose I'll hit up Josh and Caleb and Nathan. One of them should know. Caleb was a captain before he got out. He's from this kind of life.

I'm not sure what to make of this invitation. I don't want to work for the banks or the families that are tied into them. I want to do something...something that matters. I miss the army. The sense of purpose that I had. Now I'm just a college student like everyone else. My soldiers aren't calling me with their problems in the middle of the night. I don't get asked for advice or called to bail anyone out of jail.

When I was leaving, I couldn't wait to put all of that behind me. Shithead soldiers doing shithead things.

Now, though, I realize those were the best shitty times of my life. The stories. The memories.

Here on campus, there's nothing that compares to those times - to sitting around the ops tent at night bullshitting. Drinking bad coffee and pissing and moaning about foods we miss or the women we've left back home.

This invitation isn't for me. It's for the man LT believes I can be.

I'm not sure I can be that man. I'm not sure I can even attempt it.

I don't want to let him down.

But I don't know what else to do.

Beth steps out of the blinding light from the foyer. Her hair is loose around her shoulders. She scans the parking lot and I take a tiny, selfish pleasure in knowing that she is looking for me. I pull out of the darkness and roll down the passenger's side window. "Hey, babe. Need a ride?"

She laughs at my failed leering attempt and it leaves a bright spot on my soul, pushing aside the darkness and worry of my thoughts.

"How was work?"

She sinks into the seat next to me with an exhausted sigh. "Interesting, believe it or not." She points to my invitation on the dash. "I've got incredible information about our interviewer on Friday."

"Don't you worry that I might get the offer instead of you?"

Her expression suggests she hasn't even considered the possibility, but I have. I can't compete with her. I won't. "I wouldn't be a very good friend if I didn't tell you what I know, now would I? You need this job as much as I do."

Because I can't resist, I lean over, brushing my lips against hers. "I think I'm going to get obnoxious and make sure that you get the job."

"Don't you dare." But she's smiling because she doesn't think I'm serious.

It's the best idea I've had since this invitation fell into my lap. Make Beth look like the obvious choice. She'll fit in perfectly in their world. "You'll be an excellent intern."

"Clearly you don't understand the rules of the intern game and how they're different for guys and girls." When I say nothing, she continues, "I'll get my ass pinched a lot, called 'babe' and 'dollface' and have to smile and nod and not make a fuss. You'll get dragged out to bars and shown the way life is for men with power."

"That sounds painfully boring. I think I'd rather get my ass grabbed."

She closes her eyes as I start the truck and drive her home. "So what interesting tidbits did you learn?"

"Well, the old man wants to bring in fresh eyes to the internship. He's tired of hiring the kids of family friends, which is how the invite was even extended to us in the first place. He's been a big donor to the business school and figures this is a way to build relationships with new talent."

"God, I love it when you talk business. I imagine you in a pencil skirt with sexy glasses lecturing a boardroom."

She smiles at me in the darkness. "What is it with male fetishes about chicks in pencil skirts?"

"I don't have a pencil skirt fetish. I have a Beth in a pencil skirt fetish. See the difference? Smart and sexy in the same package."

"You sweet talker. You're good at this."

"What's that?"

"Making a girl feel special."

I stop in front of the house. The lights are out again. It dawns on me that they're never on. I lean over, cupping her face. "That's easy. Because you are."

I kiss her now because there's nothing else in the entire world that I want to do instead. Even the insidious thoughts about the next pill take a backseat to tasting her, slow and easy. I could spend the rest of my life kissing her.

My throat locks up, and I pull away suddenly. I'm ashamed of the confusion I've put in her eyes. "Sorry," I mumble. But I don't have a good excuse for my panic. It's just there, squeezing my chest until I can barely see beyond the black spots from lack of air.

"What?" Her hand on my forearm. Gentle. Steady. A sensation of light in the bleak darkness that's trying to drag me under.

I want to tell her. About the dark. About the pain. About the pills chasing everything away. I want to tell her how alive she makes me feel.

But doing that means I have to admit how dead I've felt for so long. Since before I came home. Since before LT made me promise I'd go to school here if he got me in.

I've been underwater. Barely breathing. And with Beth, I can really feel and it is overwhelming me.

And the rest of my life suddenly doesn't seem like something heavy and thick that I have to slog through. I suddenly very much want to figure out how to really live again.

Because if there's a chance, even the slightest chance, that she might be a part of my life next week, next year, then I...

I've got to get my shit together.

Chapter Eighteen

Beth

For the first time since I've met him, I'm worried that there is more to Noah than he's letting on. I'm tired and keyed up all at once. I walk home, unafraid on familiar streets, listening to music on the ancient iPod that Dad bought me five years ago. It's pretty much only good for music these days. They stopped updating this version a year or so ago.

But right now, I need the music to tune out the worry.

Dad left the light on for me. That's a good sign. I'm hopeful for the first time in forever. Maybe I've got a shot at this internship. Paid internships are so rare, they're like a rainbow-colored unicorn. The fact that they're recruiting juniors and not seniors...everything about this feels like it's in the too-good-to-be-true category. I've learned a lot of hard lessons about that sort of thing over the years.

Like the guy who promised he loved me for me. Until I showed him the house I shared with my father. Until he saw the reality of the life I had no intention of running away from. I would not abandon my dad. I hate even thinking about him. I've put him in the same category as Voldemort – he who shall not be named.

He abandoned the relationship so fast my head spun. Abby had been my rock during that harsh episode. She'd set me up with one of her friends, but the chemistry hadn't been there. Add in that her friend had been gay and trying to make me feel better - the whole thing had been a disaster. But I still loved Abby for trying. And Graham had become a close friend.

My dad is awake but things aren't great. The vodka bottle is on the counter.

The light is on in the bathroom.

"Dad?"

"Yeah."

I'm suspicious. He doesn't sound like he's half in the bag, but there had been a lot more vodka than what's left.

He steps out of the bathroom. He's moving fine.

"What the heck was in that shot?"

"I don't know but I haven't felt like this in years." He's smiling, really smiling.

The kind of idiot smile I wear when I think about Noah. "Dad, are you seeing someone?" I ask slowly.

He rotates his jaw for a moment, considering his words. "Not exactly. Remember the nurse from the other night?"

The hospital is a blur of forms and of placating faceless nurses and orderlies. "No?" I'm confused and it's not a feeling I'm enjoying.

"Anyway, she came by to check on me yesterday after you left for school."

"A nurse. Made a house call. What is this? Dr. Quinn?"

I'm irritated, and I can't explain why. I should be happy my dad is feeling better. Even happier that someone stopped by and checked on him. But it's not sitting right. I can't summon anything but wariness about what's going on. I've been taking care of my dad for as long as I can remember. This...this feels like loss.

I'm just tired. I shouldn't be overreacting like this. I just need sleep and everything will be better in the morning.

But he continues, and the story gets even more fantastic.

"Anyway, Sally came by and checked on me. And we went to lunch since I was actually upright and mobile." He runs his hand through his hair. "She came by tonight, and we had a couple drinks."

My dad is acting like a goofy kid, and I'm the overprotective parent. I want to switch roles. I want to be the kid he worries about. "I was worried when I saw the alcohol.

That maybe the shot had worn off."

He stills then. "It's only a matter of time, isn't it?" He scrubs his hands over his face. "Maybe it'll stick until my appointment."

"If you have the appointment."

"Here's hoping."

I swallow the lump of emotion in my throat and cross the room, hugging him quickly.

"You okay, sugar bear?"

"I'm fine, Dad. I've got an event I've got to go to Friday. I'm interviewing for a paid internship." I don't tell him that it's a big deal. I don't want to get his, or more accurately *my*, hopes up.

"You'll knock it out of the park. I'm sure of it." He kisses the top of my head. I want to tell him about Noah. I want to ask him what I should be worried about with Noah being a soldier.

But instead, I just stand there and hug my dad. Because moments like this are too fleeting, and I'm always afraid that today might be the last day I'm with him.

I can't explain my fear. It's not rational. It's not something I can turn off.

But I remember the first time I almost lost him. The day I realized that I had to be the adult in our family because the pain overwhelmed him.

It's a terrible thing to call 911 on your dad.

So when the good days come, I hold onto them with everything I am. Because I know that they're not going to last.

I crawl into bed later and grade the assignments from the stats homework. Our neighbor's Internet connection is working tonight. Some days I can access it, other days I can't. Tonight is one of the good nights. Otherwise, I would have to wait to get the campus WiFi.

Grading circles my thoughts back to Noah and the nagging worry that something is off. Maybe it's just me being paranoid.

But it isn't. He pulled away. He'd been sweet and funny one moment, and the next, he'd been distant. Not cold, exactly, but the warmth I'd expected from him was gone.

I wish my phone would ring. I don't care that I'm over my minutes for the month; I just wish he would call. Wish I could hear his voice and he would make me laugh like he did the other night.

Something changed tonight, and I have no idea what that means for our relationship.

Or if there will still be a relationship tomorrow.

Noah

It's hell knowing that you're hurting someone you care about. I saw the worry in Beth's eyes last night when I left her. The confusion that I, and I alone, was responsible for.

So when I cancel our appointment for tutoring today, I know there are a thousand and one unanswered questions I'm leaving in the void.

When I call, the school clinic to set up an establish care appointment, I am shocked that they can get me in today. Guess that's what happens when you live in an area known for one of the highest doctor-to-patient ratios. Beats the hell out of calling Womack down at Bragg and waiting six weeks for an initial appointment.

My hands are shaking by the time I get screened and led back to the doctor's office. The nurse has me strip down to my boxers and put on one of those thin paper gowns that are supposed to preserve your dignity. I sit on the exam room table for what feels like forever, and my anxiety is one heartbeat away from a full-blown panic attack.

My meds are out in the car. I'd doubled up, but it doesn't feel like that was enough.

The antiseptic smell of the doctor's office isn't as overpowering as it is in a hospital, but it's enough to trigger a waking nightmare.

I'm sweating by the time the doctor walks in. She's a short, muscular Asian woman who I'd swear was fresh out of medical school.

"You don't seem like you're doing so hot," she says in a heavy accent. It sounds like something out of New York. "Want to tell me what's going on?"

There's a nurse, but I can't tell you when she came into the room. My vision has zeroed down to a tunnel, focused on the doc.

"I don't do so well in doctor's offices," I manage. I clear my throat hard. Again. It doesn't help. I can't get enough air in my lungs.

She murmurs something to the nurse. "Are you taking anything for anxiety?"

"Klonopin." My brain, at least, has that information readily available.

"When is the last time you took it?"

My brain scatters, searching for the information. It's noon. I know that because I'm supposed to be with Beth right now. Instead, I'm freaking the fuck out in the doctor's office. "First thing this morning. Six, I think." Ballpark, anyway. I don't tell her I took two, though. That I keep to myself.

Then next thing I know, a small plastic cup is being pressed into my hand. A tiny white pill rattles in the bottom of it. The medication dissolves on my tongue. The silence in the room is heavy and thick and awkward. I'm a goddamned disgrace. LT would be so fucking proud of the kid he helped get into one of the top schools in the country shaking like a shitting dog in front of a doc.

All because I got a little banged up downrange.

Jesus.

The panic recedes, leaving the anger in its place. I'll take the anger. I can use the anger. The panic shuts everything down and makes me useless.

"So, want to talk about what happened?" The doc speaks slowly and quietly.

"That's kind of the reason I'm here." I can't talk now. My thoughts are no longer racing. My hands are steady now. "I want to figure out how to get some stuff straightened out."

"What kind of stuff?"

I shift and pull the hospital gown off my shoulders. I know what the scars look like. I know the muscles beneath them still burn most days, some days worse than others.

I know exactly what the nightmares feel like. The trapped feeling as the fire melts my uniform into my skin.

The doctor's fingers are cold where I can feel her touch. There are a lot of dead nerve endings there now.

Beth hasn't seen my shoulder. I managed to keep them hidden in the dark and the shadows that night at my place. It had been all about her. I'm glad, because despite my best efforts at convincing myself that I'm fine, that I've left the war behind, I am clearly not fine. Not by a long shot.

"The tissue has healed well. How's your range of motion?"

I zone out now. Her questions bounce off the haze of the anxiety meds. Answer all of them on autopilot as she tests my motor skills, my strength. My left arm isn’t as strong as my right. It probably never will be again, no matter how hard I work on it.

"You reported you're still taking Tramadol for pain as well as Ambien for sleep and Klonopin for anxiety. Anything else?"

My mouth is dry. I'm not sure if I can find the words I need. They're stuck in the base of my throat, right behind my Adam's apple.

"I..." I swallow again. "I need to...are there different meds I can take?" A deep breath that doesn't fill my lungs. "I don't like how I feel on them."

"And how is that?"

Dead. Numb. Like I'm running through life at the bottom of a pool of Jell-O. "Just not myself," I say instead. Because saying any of those things would have triggered a trip to the funny farm with the military. In the past, any mental health problems that escalated and were reported to the docs were dealt with quickly. Usually they got the individual sent out of the unit and the force.

We needed deploying fighters, not people sitting on the shrink's couch.

God, but I wish I'd sat on that couch. Just once. Just to get an azimuth check. Was I still normal? Would I ever be again?

"I think we need to assess whether the benefits you receive from these medicines outweigh the risks."

It's not an answer I want to hear. Some docs will do anything to keep from prescribing medication. Others are pushing pills on you the minute you walk through the door.

I leave with a fresh prescription ready to be filled.

I have referrals to a pain clinic. And the burn clinic. And the psych clinic.

Fucking great.

I should have gone to Stats. I probably would be feeling less crazy.

Chapter Nineteen

Beth

I'm in that weird space that's not a breakup, but the fresh and shiny newness is dull and damaged.

I'm tender today. I know in my heart that Noah wasn't lying about the doctor's appointment, but I can't shake the feeling that something is very, very wrong.

"Don't tell me the honeymoon is already over?" Abby leans forward in the mirror, dabbing her index finger beneath one eye.

My hands are tight in my lap, my fingers twisted together. "I'm not sure."

She turns and leans against the sink. The small bathroom we use to change for work is empty except for us.

I'm not sure I want to talk about it. I'm not sure what to say. We didn't have a fight. There was no disagreement. We were fine and then between one moment and the next, we weren't.

"Have you talked to him?"

I shake my head. "He canceled his tutoring today."

"Is he sick?"

"I don't know."

She folds her arms over her chest and makes a *tsk*ing sound. "I never figured that you'd fall this hard this fast."

"I'm not sure falling is what happened."

"Sure it is. He's missed one day with you, and you're acting like someone just stole your puppy and threatened to sell it on eBay."

I smile, if only to try and get the subject changed. "So can I ask what you've got planned for me Friday?"

"What's your favorite color?"

"Black tie doesn't exactly scream color options."

"Something sophisticated. I think a deep emerald green would be an amazing color on you."

"Abby, at this point, I'll be happy to not look homeless."

She beams at me in that impish way that tells me she has a plan. If I didn't know her better, I'd be worried, but Abby's plans always have a way of working out. I don't know if it's her constant optimism or just plain good luck, but she's definitely got a knack for miracles.

I'm not worried about what she's going to come up with. No, I'm distracted by thoughts of a guy that has taken my world and turned it inside out.

My shift goes by in a blur. I smile and make all the appropriate conversation, but my mind is a million miles away. I want to leave and call him. I want to know if he's okay.

There is a part of me that hates him for making me worry. But I don't have that claim on him.

That knowledge hurts more than his distance. The knowledge that I let my heart trip over the line and fall for him before I even knew what was happening. It's too fast, too abrupt.

It's too much everything. I don't know what to do with the aching want inside me.

The emptiness knowing that he's out there and not with me tonight. When did this happen? When did I become this needful thing craving just a note, a text, something that tells me he's okay? That it's all in my head and everything is okay?

I want to rewind everything and start over. I want to go back to that first stats session and set down clear boundaries. I don't care if I miss out on the blindingly powerful attraction or the brief moments of peace I've found with him.

I don't want the hurt. And this hurts.

My shift ends. Abby hands me a card with a list of things I need to bring tomorrow and tells me to meet her at her place at four with my black patent leather pumps.

"Hey." She stops me before we step into the darkness. She rides the bus home and her stop is in the opposite direction from where I'm heading. "I'm sure everything is fine. Maybe it's just school stuff."

"You're defending him?" I'm surprised because she's usually the first one to tell me to kick anyone not worthwhile to the curb.

She shrugs. "I've never seen you like this." She leans forward and gives me a quick hug. "I'd like to see you catch a win for once. You work so hard for everything you've got. Maybe I was hoping this would be easy for you."

Her words make my throat close off. Like we're already sitting around toasting the demise of another relationship that failed to get off the ground.

She disappears into the dark, and I stand there a moment, letting her words wrap around me. They were meant as a compliment, but they don't feel like it.

I tuck my hands into my pockets, peering up at the sky. Only the brightest stars pierce the city lights. My heart sinks a little in my chest.

I start down the sidewalk. It's damp, and there's a chill in the air. The perfect melancholy night.

A shadow moves from the darkness and takes shape, stepping into the light.

I stop breathing. He's okay. But then I see him, really see him and realize that no, he's not okay. He's alive. He's standing there.

But he is not okay.

And I don't know what he's going to tell me that will make it better, but I hope that I'm strong enough to deal with whatever it is.

Noah

I wish I didn't see the hundred thousand emotions flash across her face. At least half of them are different shades of hurt.

"I'm the world's biggest asshole." It's a hell of a greeting, but it's the only thing I can come up with.

She offers me a sad smile. I suppose I deserve a lot worse.

I toe the cement in front of me, wishing I could come up with some grand speech to explain myself. Something that would make her understand and bypass the pity I never wanted to see in her eyes.

"Nah," she says. "As assholes go, you're a relatively small one."

I smile despite myself. I want to approach, but I'm stuck to the pavement. I had a plan about what to say when I saw her. A brilliant explanation for being a dick.

"I know I don't deserve it but would you come with me?" I suck in a deep breath. "There's something I need to show you."

She starts to shake her head. I step into her space then. Rest my hands on her shoulders. "Please, Beth? Trust me just this once?"

She presses her lips together in a flat line. She's going to leave. She's going to say no. My fucking psychosis has broken us before we even had a chance.

She breathes out. A surrender. "Okay."

I start to speak, then decide against it. Instead, I lead her to my car. She sits quietly as I drive us away from campus toward my place. Her arms are folded over her middle. Protective.

I can't say that I blame her.

There's no moon tonight. There's silence but for the crunch of our feet on the gravel walkway to my front steps.

I close the front door behind us.

She's standing in my tiny kitchen. Waiting.

The light over the stove creates dim shadows in the tiny space. I stand there for a moment, uncertainty a live thing in my belly. Knocking my fist against the counter, I finally start unbuttoning my shirt.

"Noah."

I can't speak. I don't stop, though. Button after button, I strip away the protective barrier. The shield that hides my body from the world. From her.

I know the moment she sees the damage. I hear the sharp intake of breath and the silence that follows. I know what it looks like. I've seen it, of course, but only when I was really fucked up and able to stand the sight.

I can't look at it sober. At least not as sober as I am right now, which is somewhat more than normal. Without the haze of drugs, the scars bring back all the memories, the smell of burned skin, the terror and panic ripping through me as my body burned.

I want meds now. I'm physically craving the release from the fear twisting in my guts.

I suck in a trembling breath. I don't know what I'm going to say until the words start.

"I want to fucking forget the goddamned war." A heavy pause. "I came home. I want to pretend it never happened. That I'm just another college student with nothing to worry about but how to pay for school." I close my eyes. I can't see her looking at me. She deserves to know everything, but even now, exposed and vulnerable, the entire truth remains locked in my throat. "I want to forget it, but it's carved into my skin. For the rest of my life, I will carry this with me."

I'm terrified of turning around. I can't do it. The fear is raw and cutting and slices through any bit of sanity I've scraped together since I left the army and the war behind.

I feel her a moment before her hands connect with my skin. Her gentle, soft palms are flat against my back.

And then I feel it.

The press of her lips above the damaged skin of my shoulder blade. Her hands slide over the thick scars on my shoulder and bicep. A soothing caress as she finally folds her fingers over my heart.

"If this was supposed to scare me, you'll have to do better than that." Her words are a whisper across the good skin on my back.

A ragged sound escapes me. Something that might be a laugh or a sob. I don't know. I'm folding her in my arms, burying my face in the softness of her hair. Relief shudders through me, powerful enough that my eyes burn with it. I can't tell her everything. I can't.

But she's here. She didn't run away. There's no pity or revulsion in her eyes, or any emotion in between.

She put her hands on my scars, and goddamn if that didn't heal a piece of my damaged soul. I want to give her everything. My heart. My life.

Everything but the truth. I can't. Not yet. Maybe, just maybe, I can change what the truth is before I have to tell her about it.

She cups my face. Her palms are cool and soothing against the fire beneath my skin. I want to say something profound. Something meaningful that she'll remember for the rest of her life.

But she kisses me. Her lips are soft and warm and moist. She sucks gently on my bottom lip. I'm ragged enough that I can do nothing beneath the sensual slide of her tongue against mine. She shifts and her body is flush with mine. Her hips rock slow and sensuously against me, driving me wild with her tiny rhythmic movements.

"You scared me," she whispers against my lips.

My fingers clench against her back. "I'm sorry." I'll probably do it again, but I'm selfish enough to want to keep her with me for one more night.

I don't think. I lift her against me and she wraps her thighs around my hips. The pressure against my erection is pleasure and pain all at once. I want her naked against me. I want to feel her body beneath me. I want mine to tell her everything that she is to me.

I stumble to the bedroom, and we fall into the bed. There is no finesse tonight. There is simply tearing clothing and lips and hands on skin.

And then I'm there, her thighs wrapped around my hips. She's naked and beautiful beneath me. She slides her hands up over the damaged skin on my chest and shoulder to pull me down. Her mouth opens beneath mine and she urges me home.

She's sweet and wet and swollen and ready. I've somehow managed a condom, and then she's squeezing me, welcoming me, her body tense and tight and the sweetest sensation.

I slide from her warmth then back again. Smooth and slow. Her fingers find mine and our hands are bound like our bodies. Palm to palm, skin to skin, the erotic friction burning her into my soul. Her release starts as a tremble, something deep and quiet, building with gasps and that sound I love. I kiss the spot on her throat as she comes apart beneath me and I join her, tearing apart at the seams that are barely holding me together.

Chapter Twenty

Beth

His heart beats slow and steady beneath my cheek. My own heart nearly drowns out the sound. I don't know what to say to him.

What is the right response when someone shows you what war has done to their body? *I'm sorry* feels trite and insufficient. *Does it hurt* is just stupid and cruel.

What do I say that isn't patronizing or self-indulgent?

I press my lips to his heart. "I'm glad you made it home," I finally whisper. Because I've got no other words that come close to the turmoil of emotions twisting inside me.

He goes still beneath my hand. "I don't know what to say to that."

I lean up so I can see his face. There is misery and fear there - uncertainty and terrible, terrible pain. I cup his cheek. "You don't have to say anything."

He frowns a little. "I never really thought about it like that."

He shifts and pulls me close once more. I go willingly into his arms. It's so much more poignant and special after the day I've spent filled with worry for this man.

There is more he isn't telling me, but tonight, I've seen what it cost him to show me the damage the war has done to his body. I can only imagine the depth of the scars I cannot see.

It has taken so much for him to trust me with this. I see that now, and I understand so much more about the man in my arms.

My eyes burn. Before I fell for him, I wouldn't have considered being where I am at this exact moment. I would not have let myself fall for a soldier, a man damaged by an unnecessary war. I hated the war before because of what it did to my father. I hate it more now that I've seen what it did to Noah.

My father hates the weakness in his body, and he is a grown man. Noah is my age. Guys our age are busy trying to hookup at parties and going to games and living it up.

But not Noah. It's like the war has robbed him of his youth. He is older than his years, the weight he carries heavier than anything I can imagine.

My body warms again and without thinking, I slip my thigh over his hips, sliding up until I'm straddling him. His eyes widen slightly. His hands rest gently on my hips, caressing my thighs. I slip over him, surprised to find him hard again. My body is slick and wet and ready for him. I slide over his length, the gentlest erotic friction. His stomach clenches as I rock over his erection.

He presses a condom into my hand. My hips are moving now against him, a riot of sensations against my swollen heat driving me, driving him, wild with unmet need.

Slowly, I roll the condom into place. His hips jerk as I shift back, the tip of his erection poised just there. I wait until he meets my eyes. Watching, watching, I slowly, so slowly, slide down his length. Inch by inch, I take him inside me. He fills me, satiating the emptiness inside me. He's deep, so deep, inside me. I rock gently, using my body to clench around him.

His gasp is enough to drive me closer to the edge. His fingers dig into my hips, urging me to move faster.

I dig my nails into his skin, anchoring myself against him as I lift my hips and then press my body against his again. He groans, and it's the sweetest sound. I want this. I want him. Harder. I want him to take control. To pound into me until he can feel everything I feel when I'm with him.

We roll and he's there, driving into me, sending me spiraling wide. I reach between us, my fingers finding the exact spot I need and I'm coming again, violent and powerful. A scream tears from my throat and he captures it. The waves crash over me - pulsing, pounding sensations. Powerful, so powerful.

I dig my nails into his back. Urging him, whispering nothing and everything. Telling him with my body that I'm glad he's home. That he's here and I want nothing more than to be here with him at this exact moment.

And when he comes, it's a storm, a powerful release that touches the part of my soul I have tried to protect.

I'm open now, exposed and vulnerable. With a word, a touch, Noah can destroy me. There are no words for what he's done to me. I've fallen and fallen hard for this man.

There is nowhere I would rather be.

Noah

Her body trembles a little when she's in that space between sleeping and waking. I need to get her home, but I don't think I can move.

I'm broken. The stone around my heart has been shattered. It's in her hands now. There's nothing I can do to take it back.

I'm not sure I want to.

She's seen the damage. She knows at least part of what the war has done to me, and she's stayed. I'm so fucking grateful and overwhelmed, I can't speak.

I kiss her forehead. She makes a sleepy noise and nestles closer. I love the feel of her body against mine. She makes that sound again. I almost hope she's asleep and I can keep her with me.

I want to fall into her arms tonight, not Princess Ambien. There's no magical cure for what ails me, but tonight, I have at least the faintest sensation of sleep reaching up and pulling me under without the sleeping pills dragging me down first.

To sleep, really sleep, is a temptation I'd forgotten how to crave.

But I don't know how to ask her to stay. I can't tell her I need her. It's not fair to put that on her. Maybe someday.

Maybe after I talk to the docs, I'll find another way. And maybe, her dad will be well enough one of these nights that she'll stay.

But I can't ask that of her. I can't - I won't - make her choose between her father and me. I'll make sure she gets home. Because I might be crazy, but I have a little bit of honor left in me.

"I hurt you," I whisper. "I'm sorry."

She slides her palm down until it's resting over my heart. I cover it with my own. The contrast between our hands is stark. Hers have committed acts of caring, of love and devotion. Mine, acts of war. I have been cruel, and not just to the enemy. To Beth, to someone I care about more than breathing.

"Please say something. Tell me to fuck off and die or something."

She smiles and makes that sound. "I'm not going to tell you to fuck off and die." A quiet pause. "I don't know what to say. I worried about you."

"You shouldn't have."

Her expression tells me I'm a moron. "It doesn't exactly work that way, you know. I don't get to shut this off when we're not in bed."

"I know."

"Then don't do that again. Don't leave me worrying about you. Because I'm not wired like that. I can't turn it off with a snap of my fingers or a click of my heels." There is an edge beneath her words. Anger and hurt, that she's lashing back to spare me.

It does something funny to my heart to know that she is holding back again. Still. Maybe she always does. Except when she is beneath me. Then there is no holding back. Nothing restrained.

I close my eyes, unable to meet her gaze when I say what I have to say. "Maybe this is a mistake. Because, clearly, I'm still fucked up from everything. I can't promise that I won't hurt you again." I clear my throat. "You should be with someone who won't put you through that."

She shifts, and I'm afraid to see her climbing out of bed.

Walking away. Even though I'm giving her permission, the idea of her walking away breaks me a little.

"Did you hurt your brain coming up with that bullshit?" I open my eyes, and she's staring down at me, anger flashing in hers. "Because that took more creative reasoning than some of the stuff you came up with when we were starting stats."

The words are stuck at the bottom of my throat.

"You don't run when things get a little bumpy. That's not how life works. You stick. If you care about people, you stick."

I swallow the lump that's making it hard to breathe. "I'm not very good glue."

"No, you're more like two-sided tape, only one side is covered in cat litter."

I laugh and pull her close because her analogy makes no sense.

"My mom left as soon as she realized what life with my dad was going to be like. She left both of us." Hurt laces through those words, old mixed with new. I realize what I've done to her in the last day. "I will never be like her. I will never bail on the people I care about."

There's danger there - a commitment to an ideal that will only lead her to a broken heart, or worse, a burned-out broken spirit. The world has a way of doing that to even the very best of us. Especially to the best of us.

"My dad hit my mom. He wasn't a drunk or anything. He was just mean. He wanted things done a certain way, and when they weren't, he was like a giant spoiled baby." I sigh because dredging through these memories hurts more than it should. It's been five years since I last went home, and I have no intention of ever going back there. "I think she stayed for me. But now that I'm gone, I can't figure out why she stays." A deep breath. "I tried to get her to leave him when I left home. I told her I'd send her money. I'd get her set up in a place on her own. She didn't have to stay with him anymore." Beth's body tenses and she shifts, nestling closer. "She just patted me on the cheek and said I didn't understand. And she's right. I don't understand. I don't understand why someone stays in something like that."

"Maybe you should ask why he hits instead of asking why she stays." A cautious statement. One filled with wariness and resignation. Because neither question gets at the desired end state of my mom being away from my dad.

"I never thought about it that way."

She shifts then, hooking one leg around my hip and drawing me closer once more, and there's no more discussion. I need to take her home. But I'm losing myself in her once more before I face the loneliness of spending the rest of my night alone.

Chapter Twenty-One

Beth

It's strange without my dad at home. I can't explain how it makes me feel that he's not only on his feet, but also on a date. He knows I won't be home tonight. It's Friday and tonight is the big invitation-only event that has the potential to change my life - barring any natural disasters, broken shoes or slips of the tongue that result in all of us being embarrassed.

I set my bag with my expensive shoes on the floor and rifle through the mail, sorting between junk and bills. Some of them are medical, others from school.

I should have sorted them better. My hand shakes as I open the first one and absorb the amount. The miracle injection for my dad's back has set us back another seventy-five hundred dollars. Anesthesia. Blood work. Various tests. The actual injection itself was only a grand. All the ancillary stuff that went along with it that jacked up the price. It is goddamned criminal that they charged the people who can least afford to pay the highest rates.

It's not like I've been even making progress on the previous eighty thousand in medical debt, but for some reason, this number breaks me a little more. It's so much money. In the rational part of my brain, I know there are jobs out there. That I'll start paying it back once I'm working full-time.

But right now, it's more weight added to the stack of bills that are an albatross around my neck. Sometimes, everything feels like an uphill climb. I put it away and head out to catch the bus to Abby's.

I don't know what to expect tonight. Abby will have more information for me, but I've never been good at the social scene where I'm expected to interact and not simply take people's orders. I can manage in the classroom well enough, and I can smile and work the floor really well at the country club. I've paid enough attention to how the ladies who lunch act at social events; I'm pretty sure I can pull it off.

But I've never had a job hanging on a social function before. Maybe that's how these things are really decided. Who fits best, not just at the office but after work, too. I have no idea, honestly.

I try to put it out of my mind, but my stomach is in knots, twisting and turning until I'm positive that the first thing I eat is going to come right back up on me.

But then I'm at Abby's and she's pinging off the walls with excitement. It's hard not to catch her energy.

"Put this on." She hands me a deep emerald green sheath dress that looks at least three sizes too small.

"There's no way this is going to fit."

"Trust me." She ignores me while she's digging in her makeup bag. And by makeup bag, I mean small suitcase full of a billion different palettes.

The dress slides over my hips like crushed silk. It clings to my curves, but she's right - it fits like a dream. The scoop neck accents my collar bones but keeps slipping and exposing my bra. The long sleeves give it a more sophisticated feel than had it been cap-sleeved.

"Here." Two pieces of double-sided tape and she's fixed the bra problem. I step into my shoes and immediately tower over her. She pauses and glances up and down my entire length. "I knew it."

"Where on earth did you get this?"

"I have a friend who works for a place that helps women dress for job interviews."

"Who wears something like this to a job interview?" The dress is fantastic and well beyond my price range.

"Depends on the job, now doesn't it?" Abby smiles and

holds up a palette next to my face. "Sit. No peeking until I'm done."

"You are just full of commands." The butterflies in my stomach are more from excitement than nerves now.

"I'm doing a strong eye and everything else will be neutral."

"I don't even know what that means," I say.

"You'll see. And we need to pull your hair up. I want a messy bun at the base of your neck."

"That's how I do it for school."

"It ought to be easy then, huh?" She's focused now. The tip of her tongue is pressed to the corner of her mouth. "Close your eyes." I comply and try not to laugh at how serious she is at the moment. She pats and taps my face. "Did you fix the things with lover boy?"

"I think so." I'm not sure what to say. How to explain what happened last night. I know now what I'm dealing with, at least a little more. But I'm wary where I wasn't before. I want to guard my heart even though it's far too late for that.

"That is the most tepid response I've ever heard in my life."

"It's complicated."

"When isn't it? Try me."

"He's...trying to deal with some stuff from the war." It's a dodge, but his wounds are not mine to share freely. Given how hard it was for him to show me, to trust me with what happened to him, I can't just tell the world.

"And that, ladies and gentlemen, is why I will never, ever date a soldier."

"It's not all bad," I say. When my dad tells me stories about when he was gone, I can hear the regret in his voice - that he misses it. To hear him talk about it, I'm always left with the feeling like there is nothing like it. It's something I'll never experience, but that doesn't mean it hasn't touched my life indirectly through my dad and now through Noah.

"No, I'm sure it's not. And I'm the last person to judge someone for their life choices. But I've got more than enough drama in my own life. I want a well-adjusted, normal, stable guy. Not someone who needs high-risk activities or guns to feel like a man."

Neither of those things describes Noah, but I'm not going to argue with her. She is skeptical of men and their motives. I can't say that I blame her. Abby is the exception that proved the rule. Her mother raised her alone and made sure that Abby was going to college. She never told me everything her mother did to provide for her, but I get the impression that it went above and beyond working two jobs.

"Okay." She brushes beneath my eye one last time. I feel her move away.

She holds up a full-length mirror, like Vanna White turning the glowing letters. Only I'm what's glowing. She's done something to accent my eyes, just a little bit, and my lips are wet with a pale gloss. I'm a princess. Someone elegant and refined and completely at home in this place.

"Wow."

I could never have pulled this off on my own. I would have done too much makeup. The dress would have been wrong.

"Abby--"

She beams her "I told you so" expression in full force at me. "I love it when I'm right." She folds her arms over her chest, smiling. "Okay, now remember, don't talk about religion, guns or politics."

I make a face. "Why on earth would religion, guns or politics come up at a business party-slash-whatever this is?"

She lifts one eyebrow. "Sugar, you're in the South."

I laugh because it's true. I just forget that sometimes.

The doorbell rings. The cab is here. I wouldn't normally use the money for one, but I can't ride the city bus in this outfit. Noah wanted to pick me up but it doesn't look good for us to arrive together. At least not for me. I want them talking to me, not wondering what I'm doing afterward with him. And maybe that's selfish and a little bit mercenary, but I need this job. Badly.

Abby gives me a quick hug. "Knock 'em dead. For your dad."

Her words are the confidence and courage that I need.

Because I am terrified of screwing this up.

Noah

I've never been good at mingling and small talk. I've always avoided it unless I was ordered to attend. When we would be forced to do mandatory fun - otherwise known as activities we "would be at" because the commander decreed it so. LT and I would stay long enough to be seen and then sneak off. That was before the war. After - well, there was no after. I came home and left the military behind.

I'm nursing a vodka tonic and pretending to care about some local scandal with the energy company. This is the stuff I should be paying attention to, but I'm distracted. Amid the wealth and opulence of the Baywater's formal ballroom, there is someone missing.

Beth isn't here yet.

We're a half hour into the thing, and she's not here.

I offered to pick her up, but she didn't want us to arrive together. It makes sense - for her, when she points out that I don't have to manage impressions of myself like she does. But I won't argue with her because her life is not mine. I think she's wrong - she's never had to answer stupid fucking questions like, "What is it like to go to war? Did you ever kill someone?" But I'm not going to press the issue with her.

My fingers tighten around the glass, and I realize that just thinking about that question is spiking my blood pressure.

Where the hell is she?

"So tell us about yourself, Noah. What are you majoring in?" The question comes from old man Morgan. He's a big man, still intimidating despite pushing sixty. He's on, at least, his third scotch, but doesn't appear to be drunk or even on his way to being drunk.

I notice things like this. I'm all for partying and getting buck wild, but I'm wary of people who crawl into a bottle in public. It says something about their decision-making capabilities. I did it once, and it was a painful lesson that I'm unable to forget. I puked on the battalion command sergeant major's Stetson, and well, I ended up on every shit detail he could find for the next six months.

Literally.

I focus on old man Morgan and the here and now. He's not the sergeant major. He's just some old dude with a shitload of money who has the potential to solve some of Beth's problems. If she would just get her ass here.

"Business ethics and decision sciences, sir."

"Ethics. Interesting. Why ethics?" He takes a sip from his drink, and I realize that he's not actually drinking.

We can smell our own, apparently. I wonder if he's noticed I'm not drinking either. Doesn't matter how much I might want to. I can't. Not if I want to maintain my composure.

"Well, sir, I was in the military, and I want to understand how we make decisions and why organizations run the way they do. What is the line between individual ethics and business decisions?"

He's watching me closely. I want to scan the room once more, but I don't. I'm focused completely on my audience. "Do you think businesses need ethics?"

"I do, sir. I know it's not a popular field among some of our colleagues, but I believe we have an obligation to consider facts beyond profit and loss."

There's a glimmer in his eye, and I can't tell if I've pissed him off or sparked his curiosity. "Like what?"

"Like our employees. In the army, I had a lieutenant who always used to talk about second and third order effects. Not the direct consequences of our decisions, but the ones that came after that we didn't foresee."

His eyes crinkle at the edges. "This lieutenant sounds like he was pretty smart for a lieutenant."

I smile at the memory. "It drove my commander crazy that LT was smarter than he was and not just book smart. He had this way of seeing the world that was really different, but he fit, too." I find old man Morgan watching me closely and the scrutiny is a little unnerving.

"You admire him."

"Very much so, sir. I want to be like him when I grow up."

Morgan laughs, and in the space between one moment and the next, I notice Beth standing in the doorway. She's wearing something that hugs her curves. She is stunning. Glamorous and sexy and professional all at once. Her hair is twisted at the base of her neck in that way that drives me over the fucking moon wild.

Morgan notices her. Hell, everyone in the room notices her. I clear my throat. "Sir, may I introduce Beth Lamont. She's --"

He cuts me off as Beth approaches. "I've seen you somewhere before. Where?"

She flushes and the effect is stunning. "Sir, I waitress part-time here."

He frowns at her. "You say that like it's something to be ashamed of."

Her throat moves as she swallows. I want to taste every inch of her exposed skin. "No, sir. I've worked very hard to be where I'm at."

"You should be proud of that," he says to her.

She's not bristling, but it's a close thing. Morgan glances between us. "And how do you two know each other?"

"She's my statistics tutor," I say before she can come up with a different story.

"Tutor, eh?"

"Yes."

"Most men wouldn't admit to needing a tutor," Morgan says. I can't tell if he's fucking with me or not.

"I learned in the army that pretending you know what's going on when you don't can get someone killed."

"No one is going to die in Stats," Beth says.

"Feels like it sometimes. Professor Blake doesn't mess around," I say.

Morgan chuckles. "Indeed, she does not. She's terrifying."

It's my turn to frown. "You know her?"

"Son, I know everyone in this school," he says, and there's an underlying note of something I can't put my finger on.

I stiffen then. I'm not his son. He turns to talk to someone else, and I feel Beth's hand on my arm. A warning. A restraint. I finally meet her eyes.

"Don't," she whispers.

"What?"

Her lips curl into a faint, teasing smile. "You know what."

I lift one brow. "Don't want me to get drunk and puke on his Italian leather shoes? It would make you look that much better."

She shakes her head, that faint smile painted in place. "I think admitting you needed a tutor took care of that," she says.

"Good. Now go talk to his son and be brilliant. You're getting this job."

The mask she has painted on flickers. Just a little, but enough that I notice it.

"What?"

She shakes her head, and the mask is back in place. She migrates to a small cluster of people including Morgan's son. She's all business, and as I watch her work, I realize that she fits in this place better than I ever could.

LT was wrong. This is not my space, and it never can be. The world these people live in isn't my world.

I don't even know why I'm here.

Chapter Twenty-Two

Beth

I'm exhausted from being on all evening. It's a different kind of emotional drain than waitressing. You get a break between customers. You can take the fake smile off your face as you're fetching food and ordering drinks from the bar. But at a thing like this, you're on one hundred percent of the time.

My face hurts from smiling so much. My feet are ready to chop themselves off at the ankle and go on strike.

But it's over now. I've timed my departure to be right in the middle. Not the first out the door, not the last.

I didn't get to talk to Noah the rest of the evening, but I'm worried about him. He's seemed tense and strained since the night started and he looked more stressed as the night wore on. As I leave, I notice he's already gone. I try to ignore the disappointment. I wanted to talk to him. To see if he was okay.

I step outside and walk to the end of the building to call a cab. No point in advertising the fact that I don't have a car. Well, I do, but it's not the kind of car you drive to an event like this. Our fifteen-year-old Buick doesn't exactly fit in with the shiny BMWs and Mercedes'.

I feel him before I see him. He melts from the shadows. Relief is a palpable thing across my skin.

"Hey." He's tired, but there's something else.

"Hi," I say.

"Are you rushing home?"

I shake my head. "My dad has a date."

"Really?"

"Yeah."

"Last emergency room visit ended up being a good one, huh?"

"That was the night I called you. It wasn't a good one." I shrug. "But yeah, I guess the shot they gave him that visit made a big difference."

"You don't seem happy about it."

I follow him to his car, grateful that he's here. That he waited for me. That things feel closer to normal than they had. "I guess I'm waiting for the other shoe. We've had spells like this before, and they never last."

He opens the door for me. He's close, right there. I can reach out and touch him if I want. And I want to. Badly. I slide my hands beneath his jacket. His shirt is warm and I want to strip away the barriers between us.

"That's pretty cynical for someone so young."

His mouth is there, just there. I brush my lips against his, needing his touch, his taste. "Not cynical. Realistic."

My hands are wandering over his chest. I can't get enough of him. I'm edgy and needy, and I suddenly very much want to be alone with him.

"Well, Realistic, would you like a ride home?"

I step closer until my body brushes against his. "I'd like something."

"Did I tell you how amazing you look this evening?"

"Abby is my fairy godmother."

"Do you turn into a pumpkin at midnight?"

I'm slowly untucking his shirt, grateful that he's parked in a dark side of the lot away from the lights and the parking lot security cameras and the rest of the world.

"I think the coach turned into a pumpkin at midnight." His stomach is hot and smooth. I run my thumb over the edge of his hip bone and feel his belly jump beneath my fingers.

He captures my face in his hands, his eyes intense. He opens his mouth like he's going to say something, but he kisses me instead. I sigh into him, relief and need twisted and achy inside me. His tongue slides against mine, teasing, stroking.

Burning me up with sipping, sensual licks. He nibbles on my bottom lip before sucking gently on the spot.

"Stay with me?" A plea.

My breath gets caught somewhere beneath my heart. "I--"

"I'm sorry. I shouldn't have asked. You need to be home." He's kissing my jaw, then. Teasing, nibbling kisses along the pulse in my throat.

"I want to." Because I do. But I'm afraid. He sucks gently on the spot right below my ear. I'm melting for him.

"Come home with me?" He pauses then, cupping my cheeks. "If you change your mind and want to go home, I'll take you. I don't care if it's three a.m. or what." A hesitant kiss against my swollen lips. "I want to wake up with you. I want to make you breakfast and feed you."

There's an edge to his words. Something needy and a little terrifying and completely compelling. The idea of waking up with him is...it's something I haven't dared let myself want.

I don't know how tonight went. It didn't feel like a disaster, but the one thing I'm terrible at is reading people at this place.

But nothing that happened tonight feels as right, as good, as thinking about waking up with Noah.

"I don't have a toothbrush."

"There's a twenty-four hour drug store on the way to my house."

I smile at his deadpan response. "You've thought about this."

"More than you'll ever know."

Noah

She says yes.

I mean, it's a simple thing, right? Spending the night with someone. Happens all the time. But it's not a simple thing.

When she's been at my place, it's been dark. And I've been plenty distracted by the feel of her beautiful body beneath mine.

But asking her to spend the night means she'll see everything in the broad light of day. She'll see the medication in the kitchen. She'll see the scars again and maybe she'll decide that I'm not worth it.

I don't know if this is a mistake or a test. I'm known for fucking up the good things in my life. LT was always really good at stopping me from stepping on my dick despite myself. I wonder if he'd tell me to take her home to her place or mine.

I wish I could see into the future and figure out if this was either the best idea I've ever had or the worst. I carry her into my house because I can't bear to be separated from her. I want this fascinating, beautiful, loyal woman in ways I can't explain.

I don't make it very far.

I'm careful taking her dress off. Lowering the zipper, I'm enthralled by the sight of her in her panties and bra and those magnificent heels that accent her gorgeous legs. "You've got the most amazing curves."

She smiles and shakes her head. "You should talk dirty to me more often."

I step to her until she backs into my small kitchen table. Lay her back until she's spread open before me. A feast that I plan on savoring for as long as she'll let me.

"Beautiful. So fucking beautiful."

She makes that sound in her throat. It reminds me of a purr. "I want to take your panties off."

"Oh hell, you're really going to talk dirty?"

I kiss her to stop her from talking. "Shh."

She lies back, draping her arms over her head. Her breasts rise and fall with each breath. I reach behind her, unhooking that incredibly sexy black cotton. I could stand there watching her for hours. She's perfection. I frame her belly with my hands, sliding them over her soft skin to cup her breasts. Her nipples pebble beneath my touch. Her eyes darken as I stroke her skin gently. Watching her body respond is a powerful drug, a hit of the purest ecstasy.

I lean down, teasing one nipple with the tip of my tongue. The barest caress. She gasps at the slightest touch. I lick her belly, then lower. Lower. Until her sex is just there, ripe for me. I kiss her gently and feel her wetness through the cotton. She's swollen.

"I want to see you," I whisper. "I want to taste you."

A quiet moan is my reward. It's exquisite torture pulling her panties off. Seeing her drives all the blood straight to my cock. Goddamn it, she's fucking gorgeous. Swollen and glistening perfection. I stroke my thumb across the seam of her body. She whimpers, her hips jerking beneath my touch. She's slick and oh so wet.

I love her taste. I circle her with my tongue, listening to her gasps and cries to find exactly what makes her crazy. I suckle her and she digs her fingers into my hair.

Again, I suckle her. She nearly bucks me off when I slide my thumb inside her. Stroking her with my fingers, using my mouth. She's gone, over the edge. I feel her start to come on my finger. Squeezing, pulsing, she's tight, so fucking tight. I'm relentless, driving her over the edge of her orgasm.

And then I'm sliding inside her, riding the receding edge of her climax. She's tight and pulsing around me, urging me with her body, her nails, her feet digging into my ass. Demanding everything I am, everything I have.

I lift her and carry her to my bed. I'm still inside her as we tumble into my sheets. She straddles me, riding me, driving me closer, closer. I love seeing her rising over me, her hair falling down from the prim and proper bun, tumbling over her shoulders in a mess of dark blond.

And then there's no more thought as my orgasm rips through me, tearing at the remains of my soul. I pull her closer, trying to keep her there, exactly there. I want to be inside her forever.

I wait until she's falling asleep to slip from her embrace to sneak into my kitchen. I'm not foolish enough to try and sleep without the Ambien. Tonight, though, I cut the pill in half. I'm going to do this. It starts tonight. Half of what I'm used to taking.

It's worth a shot, right?

I slip back into bed. She makes a sleepy sound and curls closer. She's softness in my arms. Her hair is cool silk against my scars.

She's a peace I'll never know, but maybe, just maybe, I can reclaim a tiny piece of what I lost.

"I'm falling for you." There's no response in the darkness. I didn't expect any. The mere fact that she's here, sleeping with me, trusting me...It breaks me a little more knowing that I've lied to her.

I'm lost in her, and I don't know how to find my way out of this mess I've created.

I'm not sure I want to.

Chapter Twenty-Three

Beth

He's making me breakfast. And I'm not allowed to help. He kisses me and tells me to take a shower and he'll take me home. It's early, but I'm not tired. I slept, really slept. The worry about home is still there, it's always there, but it's not overpowering.

I step into his shower, holding my face under the steady, strong stream. His shower is tile, real tile. It's older, but that's not the point. Our shower is ancient plastic that's impossible to get really clean. And the water pressure in his shower is just this side of amazing. It beats into my skin, massaging my body with hot, wet heat.

I slip into one of his button-down shirts. It falls mid-thigh and the sleeves are too long. I roll them up and realize that I have nothing to wear home. I can't possibly put the dress back on. I'm terrified of ruining it.

I inhale the warm smell of toast.

I walk in, and his gaze sweeps down my body and back up again.

"I approve of this wardrobe selection," he says, turning his attention back to the pan.

"I'm not sure what I'm going to get home in, but I'm sure I'll come up with something."

"Grab a pair of my sweats and flip flops. I know where you live. I'll get them back, I'm sure."

Guilt sneaks up and wraps around my heart. I should have told him a long time ago about the address.

He flips the eggs flawlessly.

"Of course you can cook eggs. I always end up mangling the yolks."

"They're probably still good if you cooked them."

"That is seriously cheesy," I say. I sit at the table and butter a piece of toast. "Where did you get this bread?"

"Grocery store on Ninth Street. I splurged this week."

A luxury we have never afforded. I don't resent it. I savor the taste and texture. I used to make bread in our bread machine, but then it broke and I never got around to digging through the local thrift stores to find a new one. I should do that. Dad likes my bread.

"So what are your plans for the day?" he asks. "It's Saturday and all that."

"I've got to work today at three. Finish an assignment and prep for stats lab this week."

He slides a plate in front of me. The eggs are perfectly cooked. I pierce the yolk with my bread. "This is fantastic."

"I'm glad you like eggs. I probably should have asked first, but since you've never said anything about food issues, I guessed."

I smile up at him, and wish I could see past the blinding bright spot that Noah is in my life. Wish I could see how this ends. If it's a happily ever after or a Greek tragedy.

I slide my arms around his waist. For a moment, I simply rest my head on his shoulder and breath him in, surrounded by his warmth, his scent. Everything about him fills me with something I haven't had space or room for in my life.

And I need this now. I need him. He's a craving that only gets stronger each time I satisfy the urge. His arms come around me and he kisses my neck. It's a simple embrace. Something powerful all on its own. "I want to stay here forever," I whisper. My voice is thick. Heavy with fear that I'm afraid to give words to, afraid to put out into the universe.

His arms are tight around me, like I'm a lifeline for him as much as he is for me.

He leans back and cups my face. I love this habit of his. It's something warm and tender and incredibly erotic all at once.

"This is pretty intense for me," he says. "I never expected to fall for my hot stats tutor."

I smile because it's the corniest thing he could have said. "You weren't expecting me?"

"No one can expect someone like you, Beth." His voice is serious now. "You're a unicorn. People like you don't exist."

"I don't know what that means." I'm terrified that it means he's put me on some kind of pedestal. Elevated me to some exalted sainthood that I don't deserve.

"It means you're pretty damn special to me." He brushes his lips against mine. "And I'm terrified of fucking this up."

I nuzzle his neck because I hate the space between us. "You won't."

"Don't underestimate my powers," he says.

I laugh quietly. "I will never underestimate your power to cook delicious eggs."

"Well, I've got that going for me. Speaking of which, you should eat before they get cold."

He urges me back into my chair. My skin protests the loss of his warmth, but I eat because he cooked for me. I don't normally have a big breakfast. Some peanut butter and an apple usually does the trick for me.

This is a feast in so many ways.

He joins me a few minutes later and we sit in the morning sunshine that fills his small kitchen. I notice the torn remains of a tattoo at the edge of a scar on his upper arm.

Before I can stop myself, I trace my fingers over the jagged, raised edge of the burn.

He stiffens but doesn't pull away. His nostrils flare as he watches my fingertip slide over his skin. "What was the tattoo?"

"Tribal armband. Completely unoriginal." He lifts his arm and reveals the unrestricted remnant on the underside of his bicep. It's a mixture of flames and waves in an intricate pattern. It looks like it's solid colors, but closer inspection reveals tiny designs in each color block.

"Do you ever think about getting it redone?"

Noah

"Tattooing over scars is tricky. I'd have to find the right artist." I haven't allowed myself to go there until now. I keep the jagged remains of the tattoo as a reminder of what was destroyed on that terrible day.

I lost everything that mattered to me.

I'm not ready to cover it with new ink and pretend that I've come out on the other side all better.

"My dad has a couple of army tattoos. The Ranger tab on one shoulder. And his old unit patch."

I smile because it's something that new soldiers do all the time. And it's easier to shift the conversation to her dad than my war.

She slides my t-shirt sleeve higher, though, back to inspecting the scars and the shredded remains of the tattoo. I brace for more questions that I'm not sure I'm ready to talk about.

Maybe I need to. Maybe I need to tell her about the war, about LT and the guys. About why things feel like they fit when I'm around Josh and Caleb and Nathan. What I have with her is something different. Something that fits, too. But it's something fragile. Something I can still break.

She surprises me now, placing a soft kiss on the center of my shoulder. I can barely feel it through the damaged nerves, but the surrounding sensations remind me of what it's like to feel. Her hair brushes against my good skin. Her fingers are a gentle pressure on my forearm. She overwhelms me with that single gesture, and I'm undone by the simple tenderness of it.

I force myself to remain still. To not panic. I close my eyes, letting the sensations wash over me.

Her touch battles with the fear that threatens to unman me. The fear that has been with me since that terrible day. My breathing is ragged.

If she can sense my distress, she doesn't say. She simply slides out of her chair and into my lap and pulls me into her arms. I'm lost in an ocean of conflict. I want to be here with her, but the war won't let me go. It intrudes into every moment of peace I try to hold onto.

There's nothing I wouldn't give up to stay in this moment with her. To leave the war outside and pretend that I'm a nice, normal, well-adjusted guy.

But normal, well-adjusted guys don't have a platoon of pills lined up in their pantries. We don't lie to ourselves about being able to sleep without sleeping pills or need double doses of anxiety medication to go to the damn doctor.

I'm a fucking disaster, and I'm ruining everything with my silence. I need to tell her everything. I need to give her a chance to get out while she still can. Before she falls as hard for me as I've fallen for her.

The thought of never seeing her again - it hurts. My heart aches with the imagined loss.

I rest my head on her chest and slide my arms around her waist, holding her close. I never want to let her go.

I have to. I have to get her home. She has things to do that don't involve me.

I've got to figure out how to fill my time while I wait for her to get off her shift. I'll pick her up tonight because that's become my routine. My excuse to see her.

Because having her in my life has become as routine as breathing. I need her like I've never needed anyone, and it terrifies me that she has this power over me that I've never given freely to anyone.

I close my eyes. My hands are flat on her back, holding her, stroking her soft skin beneath my shirt.

"This is a great way to spend a morning," she whispers.

"There are no alternatives I can think of that would be better."

She makes that sound in her throat, and I can feel it beneath my cheek.

"What will you do today?"

"Homework," I say. Because it's the truth. "I'm practicing being a responsible student. I've got some stiff competition in class."

She runs her fingers through my hair. Her touch is like little electric pulses along my skin. "I've got to check on my dad," she whispers.

"I know. I'm just pretending for a moment that I don't have to take you home."

She sighs heavily. "So I need to tell you something," she says.

There's an ominous tone to her voice that sets me on edge. I wait, saying nothing.

"I don't live where you've been dropping me off." She's wary now. There's a deep concern in her voice.

She won't meet my eyes.

"Do you live in a van down by the river or something?"

She blinks - once, twice - then laughs out loud. "I used to watch old episodes of *Saturday Night Live* with my dad. I love that Chris Farley skit." She sucks in a trembling breath. I can feel her shake beneath my touch. "You're not mad?"

"Unless you're living in a crack house, in which case I'm going to be mad because you're not living somewhere safe. No I'm not mad. Why would I be?"

"Because I've been lying to you. Pretending to be something I'm not."

I cup her face then because I can feel the fear in her and I hate it. "I'm not mad. If this is the worst lie you've told me, then I think you're off to a pretty good start. You're not selling drugs to pay for school or anything illegal or otherwise?"

She gives a choked laugh. "I won't tell you I didn't think about it once or twice with my dad's bills. But he needs the medicine, so I can't really sell it."

"I thought about pretending to have ADHD once and selling the pills."

"Really?" She's mildly horrified and smiling at the same time.

"No, not really. I just wanted to make you laugh."

Because if this is the worst lie she's told, then my sins are that much worse. I think of the little sentries in my pantry, the formation of orange bottles in a regimented row. I should show her what my life is like. Show her what I hide from everyone.

But I can't. Because I'm a coward. I'm afraid to show her what the war has really done to me. How I've let a single incident take over my life. It has burned away everything, leaving me with a shadow of what was.

But I leave the pantry closed.

Because I cannot bear to lose her.

Chapter Twenty-Four

Beth

"You can come in if you want."

We're sitting in front of the tiny house I share with my dad. I see it now through his eyes, and the burning shame I feel is hot on my neck. The gate to the wire fence is hanging off one hinge. The grass died a long time ago, and I don't have the time, effort or energy to put into fixing the yard. The porch needed a new coat of paint like fifteen years ago.

I've never been embarrassed to be flat-ass broke until right now. My eyes burn with the shame of not having worked hard enough. That maybe if I'd fought with the VA more, my dad would be fixed instead of having to use the emergency room for routine care they should have provided him.

Noah's fingers slide over the back of my neck. They're warm and strong and offer instant comfort against the shame burning on my skin.

"I can practically hear you thinking over there," he says. He nudges my cheek until I'm forced to meet his gaze. "This is nothing you have to hide. Nothing to be ashamed of."

I offer a weak smile. "Get out of my head." But there's no bite to my words. I can't summon the energy. The shame is pushing me down, like an elephant sitting on my chest.

"I've done plenty of things to be ashamed of in my life. Living in a place you can afford, making sure your dad is taken care of while you work your ass off to get through a top twenty program isn't one of them."

I blink rapidly, fighting the burn. "When you put it that

way, you make me sound like Superwoman."

He brushes his lips against mine. "Maybe you are."

I shake my head. "I'm not."

He strokes my cheek with his thumb. His words have soothed the burn a little, but it's still there. Still an oppressive thing sitting on my shoulders.

"I think I'd like to meet your dad."

I am embarrassed to be wearing his clothing. My dad isn't a prude by any stretch of the imagination. He's always taught me to be responsible when it comes to sex. Still, it feels somewhat wrong to walk into the house in Noah's clothing with Noah in tow.

"I guess there's no time like the present." Because it's true. I was going to tell my dad about Noah at some point. Like today, maybe. "If he's home."

"Still not okay with the idea of your dad dating?"

"It's not that," I say. "He's done this kind of thing before. He goes all bonkers over a woman and ends up doing something stupid that sets him back."

"You have had an interesting life." He sighs. "He doesn't own any guns, does he?"

I smile at his feigned nervousness. "No. I sold them after I found him sitting up one night with a beer in one hand and his nine millimeter in the other."

"Jesus, Beth."

I shrug. "It was a long time ago. Right after my mom left us."

"Wasn't selling it illegal for you?"

"I had a friend of his from work do it."

"Shit."

I climb out of the car and wait for Noah to round the vehicle. I'm more nervous than I realized. My hands are shaking beneath the neatly folded dress draped across my arm.

I unlock the front door. The lights are off.

I slip in something wet. My heart starts pounding. Somewhere in the back of my mind, I have the foresight to put the dress down before I fall, stumbling toward my dad in the middle of the kitchen floor.

"Call 911."

But I think Noah is already on the phone.

"Dad? Dad?" There's blood beneath his face. I check for a pulse. It's there. Faint but there.

I manage to roll him over. Noah is there, helping me. "Stabilize his head and neck," he says.

I can barely see through the tears. I'm blinking and swiping at my eyes, trying to see. I slap his cheeks, trying to wake him up.

I'm vaguely aware of kneeling in broken glass. He moans and his eyes roll back in his head. From somewhere far off, I hear the wail of the sirens.

Noah pulls me away as the paramedics rush into the kitchen.

"What happened?" the short woman EMT asks as she barks commands at her partner.

"I don't know. I came home and he was face down on the kitchen floor."

"Does he have a history of alcohol or substance abuse?"

The shame is back, burning over my face. "Yes."

"Which one?"

"Both. He suffers from severe back pain, and when we run out of medication, he self-medicates with alcohol."

Such a sterile explanation for the chaos that is my life.

"What was he taking before this episode?"

"He was recently prescribed Tramadol and Flexeril instead of the Oxycodone he normally takes. He was supposed to have an appointment early next week. The ER docs refused to prescribe him Oxy."

It is in that moment that I realize his medications are all missing. They are not lined up on the counter like neat little soldiers.

Goddamn it.

The paramedic says nothing as she and her partner roll my dad onto the stretcher. He's not responding to anything they've attempted. "Are you riding with us or following?"

"Riding with you."

"No." Noah's hand on my shoulder stops me. "You're bleeding," he points out. Somehow he's managed to find me a pair of yoga pants and a sweater, along with a first aid kit. "We'll follow you."

In the car, I shrug out of his bloodied sweatpants. "I bled all over your pants."

"It's just blood. It'll come out." There's a resignation in his voice, something dark and troubled. "Make sure you've got the glass out."

My knees aren't nearly as bad as the blood suggested. There's no glass.

I change quickly because we are at the emergency room moments behind the ambulance.

I know this drill.

And I am terrified that this time, it might end differently.

Noah

I shouldn't have come here, but I couldn't leave her to face this alone. In some rational part of my brain, I know she's done this sort of thing without me before. But I couldn't leave her alone.

Instead, I'm useless and frozen in the emergency room while she talks to the admitting personnel. If I'd found a way to stay busy, I might not have noticed the smell. The underlying latent fear. Hospitals and churches are where most people confront their mortality, and it is generally an unpleasant experience.

We're not very good at facing the ends our lives.

I've already done that once before, and I'm not too keen on doing it again. But I can't leave her alone.

"He's in triage. Once he's stable, we'll send someone out for you."

"Can you at least tell me what the initial assessment is?"

"Accidental overdose."

Beth's hand covers her mouth. I'm there, supporting her as she staggers beneath the news. Supporting her is enough to keep me from falling apart myself. The panic is there, just waiting for its opportunity to strike. To turn me into a shaking ball of pathetic misery. To remind me of the temperature that melts flesh into bone.

"I've got you." I pull her against me and guide her outside because I cannot be in that waiting room another moment longer.

There are wooden benches. I guide her to one. She's limp against me as we sit. I hold her and whisper nonsense. She feels light as a feather.

"I shouldn't have left him." Words like shattered glass.

"It's not your fault."

She stiffens in my arms. "I left him."

"It's not your fault."

"I've seen that movie," she whispers. "And you're right, it's not my fault, but I knew the risks. I knew this couldn't last."

I can feel the anger rising in my chest like bile. "You're determined to blame yourself for this."

"I've been doing this a lot longer than you've known me, Noah. I know the drill, and I knew the risks." She's repeating herself. She's in shock and she doesn't even realize it.

"The risks of taking one night for yourself? One fucking night, Beth. When is the last time you've done that?" I'm not shouting, but it's a close thing. The anger is there, just there. Barely leashed.

She doesn't answer because she can't. Her eyes are rimmed with red and the sadness surrounding her is breaking my heart. She's miserable, and she's determined to pour more salt on the self-inflicted wounds.

"He was alive when we found him," I say, attempting more rational conversation. "He's going to be fine."

She covers her mouth with her hand, muffling a sob. "I can't lose him, Noah. I can't. He's the only family I've got."

The ragged pain in her voice breaks me. Reminds me that I've walked away from my family, but they're still out there in the world somewhere. Her mother is out there, but it's clear that the only family who matters to Beth is her father.

I pull her close. Her tears soak through my shirt. I don't care. I hate seeing her like this. And what's worse is that she's gone through this how many times before alone?

"They shouldn't have switched his medication," she whispers. "I don't even know what Tramadol is."

"They say it's supposedly less addictive than oxy." And that's bullshit, but I don't tell her that. She doesn't need to know about my problems today.

Of course, if I freak the fuck out in the middle of the ER, she's going to figure out everything a hell of a lot faster than I want her to. I can handle this. I have to.

I can't leave her alone. No one should have to put their father in the hospital.

Part of me hates the man who has Beth's devotion. He should have been a better fucking man and figured out his medical problems. He should have gotten off his ass and fought. Instead, he's laid around and let Beth take over running both their lives. He was a goddamned soldier, damn it. He should have fought harder.

My eyes burn. I hate him for doing this to her. He's turned his little girl's love into something he can lean on when he's too stoned to take care of himself. And Beth - goddamn her, she doesn't even see it. He's not going to get better. He doesn't have to because she'll always be there to pick up his life.

I can't say any of this to her. I admire her too much to slap her in the face with her devotion. Because that's what this is. This is a daughter who loves her father. She just can't see that her father has let her down.

I hold her. Sitting outside of my own personal hell, I stay with her. Hours pass. She calls into work and tells them she's had an emergency. Her boss gives her grief, but she fends him off with her cool, professional Beth voice.

When the nurse comes out and asks her to step into the back, I go with her.

"Your father has suffered a seizure." The doctor is brisk

and cold. Hell of a bedside manner. "We suspected alcohol poisoning and pumped his stomach. He mixed alcohol with his pain medication. We believe the Tramadol and Flexeril triggered the seizure. We're going to admit him and run some more tests."

She nods. "Is he awake?"

"He is. We're hoping you can talk some sense into him. He's trying to check himself out against medical advice."

"He's what?"

"He says he's going home. Given the scare, the likelihood of a concussion as well as possible liver damage, we're strongly advising against it."

I find her fingers, threading them into mine. She's limp, like she's given up completely. "Don't," I whisper. "Don't let him do this without a fight."

Chapter Twenty-Five

Beth

"Dad?"

He's got an IV in one arm. There's a butterfly bandage over one eye. His jaw is swollen.

He blinks, and it takes a minute before he recognizes me. "Hey, sugar bear."

"The docs tell me you're being a pain in the ass." My voice breaks and the tears start again.

"Ah hell, honey, don't cry." He holds open his arms and I lay my head on his chest. I can't help it.

"You scared me." The truth, even if it's only the partial truth.

"Not gonna lie. I scared myself this time."

His arms are limp. He can barely hold them around me.

"What happened?"

"I had a couple of drinks with Sally. Next thing I know, I'm here."

I lean back so I can look down at him. I can feel Noah standing near the door. Dad hasn't noticed him yet, but for me, he's a balm, soothing the anger and fear pulsing beneath my skin.

"All your medication is gone, Dad. Are you sure she was a nurse?"

"She was here the other night. You don't remember her?"

"I never met her, Dad." My heart hurts because he's confused. He's never introduced me to Sally. I don't know if she was here or not. And clearly neither does he. "You can't come home tonight, Dad. You have to let them check you out."

"You and I both know we can't afford it."

"You came here earlier this week and didn't have a problem with it."

"And then I saw the bill. For a couple of shots and some pills, we're in the hole another seven grand."

My heart is breaking in my chest. I'm going to lose him, and he doesn't care. "I don't care about the money." My words break. Shatter like shells on pavement.

"Well, it's time that one of us did. I can't keep doing this. We're going to lose the house at this rate."

"They can't take the house," I say. But I'm not sure.

"I'm fine. I messed up my meds or something. I'm going home."

"You're not listening to me!" Tears are falling hard down my face now. "You cannot come home. You had a seizure. You need to let them figure out what happened so it doesn't happen again. You don't have any medication, Dad."

"I've got my appointment next week. We've managed without medication before, we'll manage again. I'm not staying here tonight. It'll be another fifteen thousand at least."

"I don't care about the money!" I'm screaming at him now. "You've got to stay and let them fix you!"

"Calm down, sugar bear. You're going to get us in trouble."

Noah's arms come around me, but I push away from him. He doesn't let me go. "No, Dad. Don't tell me to calm down. I won't let you do this. You can't come home. You have to stay." A broken whisper. "Please don't do this, Daddy. Please stay." I swipe at my cheeks because I can't see. "I can't lose you. Please let them fix you. Please?"

Noah is the only thing holding me up.

"Is everything okay in here?" A security guard steps into the room, hand braced on the utility belt on her hip.

"Fine, ma'am," Noah says. She studies us all for a moment. She doesn't look convinced but leaves us be.

My dad finally notices Noah. "Who are you?"

"I'm Noah. I'm a friend of Beth's."

"Is 'friend' a euphemism for something I should be worried about?"

"I think you should be worried about taking care of your health, sir. Beth is quite capable of taking care of herself."

My dad cringes, physically recoiling from the slap in his words. Shame burns up my neck. I thread my fingers with Noah's. I appreciate the gesture if nothing else. If it takes a stranger shaming my dad into staying in the hospital, I'll take it.

"That's a low blow coming from someone I don't know," my dad says.

"Yes, sir, it is. But you didn't see how she's been breaking her back trying to take care of you. The least you can do is do your part and try to take care of yourself."

"You don't know dick about me."

"I know you were a soldier and that you got hurt during the war. Believe me, I know all about that."

"What do you know about the war? You're just some spoiled rich little fuckstick whose mommy and daddy paid his way through this place."

"Staff Sergeant Noah Warren, sir. No one has paid for anything I haven't earned."

There is curiosity in my dad's eye now. "You were in the army?"

"Got out about six months ago. I was downrange before that."

"Where?"

"Which time?"

"Last?"

"Taji. North of Baghdad."

"I know where it is. I was just outside there. Near Sadr City."

"Fun place to spend your deployment."

They've changed languages. Oh they're still speaking English, but they're talking about places I've never been. There is a meaning beneath their words now, a shared experience that I will never be a part of.

My panic recedes. Noah is talking to my dad like it is a

completely normal thing to discuss the war in a hospital emergency room. Maybe it is.

And I am amazed at the transformation, not just in my dad, but in Noah. I now see the soldier in him in a way I never saw before. He stands a little bit straighter. His body language shifts into something more regimented.

"Sir, I've only known your daughter a short while, but I've never seen anyone work as hard as she does. I'm asking you, one soldier to another, to please stay tonight. Not for yourself. For her."

"Don't call me 'sir'; I worked for a living."

Noah grins. I don't get the joke. I'll ask him to explain it later if I remember.

"Don't make her spend every waking hour worrying about you, trying to figure out how to fix you."

"Damn it, son, I get it."

"Good." Noah squeezes my fingers. "I'll wait for you outside? I need to get some air."

He leaves and but for a moment, I fall a little bit harder.

"Where'd you find him?" My dad sounds disgruntled now. I don't really care. At this point, I want him safe and not in pain.

"I'm tutoring him in stats."

"A soldier, huh?"

"He was. He's not anymore."

"Enlisted boys are trouble."

"Says the enlisted boy." No sarcasm there at all.

"You like him."

Understatement of the century, but I'm not really able to shift gears this quickly. I'm still raw and a little wounded from yelling at him. "I can't have this conversation right now, Dad."

He flushes and looks away. "So if I'm staying, could you get me a few things from the house? Toothbrush, maybe?"

The tears are back and holy hell am I tired of crying. You'd think there would be a point when you'd run dry, but no, there are always more. "I can do that."

He holds open his arms, and I go to him again because he's

my dad and he's alive and I am so fucking grateful that he is still alive today. I lay there and breathe in the smell of the antiseptic and the medical tape and his soap and skin.

Because there is nothing else I can do.

Noah

I danced a little too close to the edge in there. I wanted to stay. I needed to leave. I said my piece and got the fuck out of Dodge before I fell apart in front of both of them. And wouldn't that be just fucking perfect for Beth? Her dad ODs and then she figures out that the guy she's dating has his own issues.

I'm sitting outside on the bench. My heartbeat is slower now. Mostly back to normal. I'm not sweating anymore and my hands are steady. Mostly

I'm resting my head on my hands. Hunched over in a ball of deep breathing misery. I wish I'd taken LT up on some of that metaphysical shit he was trying out when we were downrange. He'd been dating a medic who'd been all into yoga and meditation and shit. He swore that he was sleeping better because of it. I think he was just sleeping better because he was getting some ass between patrols.

I met Katie the medic. She seemed nice. And LT had really liked her. I wonder what would have happened if their relationship had made it home.

But it hadn't, and there isn't much to do about it now, is there?

I close my eyes and wonder how Beth is doing. How her dad is. I can't go back in there, though. I'm this close to completely losing my shit, and I really don't want to do that to Beth. Not today. Hell, not ever.

Which complicates things just a little bit. How the hell do I get cleaned up when I haven't even told her that I've got a small problem with pills?

"Fuck." I sit back hard, banging my head on the bench. Stars explode in front of my vision. What the hell have I done?

She was all freaked out about telling me about her real address.

I've got to figure out how to tell her, "Hey babe, you know those scars? Well, they still fucking burn, and oh, by the way, I can't sleep without sleeping pills because every time I close my eyes, I'm back in that fucking fire. It was cool sleeping with you, but I wasn't really there. I had to get high first and pass out."

I am such a fucking loser. I scrub my hands over my face. I know what's happening. I'm far too familiar with the symptoms. Racing thoughts. Pounding heart. I'm having a full blown fucking anxiety attack in front of the hospital, and I don't have my goddamned meds.

I've lost my shit twice in the last week, and I'm not prepared for it. Because I'd stopped carrying the fucking pills with me because I'm tired of feeling like a goddamned junkie. Well, guess what, soldier boy, turns out maybe you should take a little of your own advice and take better care of yourself.

Jesus, I'm having an argument with myself.

"Hey?"

I lower my hands and see Beth standing there. She looks damaged and fragile. Like the slightest touch will send her over the edge.

"How's your dad?"

"They're doing blood work on him right now. He's a baby when it comes to needles."

She's trying to make light of it, but she's so transparent she's practically translucent.

"Let me take you home?"

She nods. Her eyes are bruised and red. I stand then and hold out my arms. She walks into them, and I almost collapse from the purest pleasure of holding her against me. She trusts me. And I have fucked things up beyond repair by lying to her from the start.

Oh, I can come up with a thousand excuses. It didn't really come up. There was no box to check on the interview for a tutor to declare drug problems and panic attacks.

Or maybe I can justify it by saying I really don't have a problem. The pills enable me to function. Isn't the definition of a problem something that interferes with everyday life? In that case, the scars and the fucking war are the problem, not the pills.

None of those explanations work, because they're all more lies surrounding the fragile truth.

I'm an addict, and I have been since I woke up from that fire with my veins full of morphine. And I've fallen for a girl whose father is an addict.

And I am going to break her fucking heart when she finds out.

I walk her to my car, and we're both silent. I don't have the energy to make small talk, and she apparently doesn't either.

Maybe I can talk to the psych doc, and she'll help me figure out a plan to get clean before I have to tell Beth the truth. Maybe I won't have to break her heart all over again.

We ride in silence. I follow her into her house. She starts to pick up the kitchen.

I stop her. "Get your dad's stuff. I'll take care of this."

She doesn't argue. I half expect her to. She moves down the hall. I find the broom and sweep up the broken glass, then mop the floor.

It's only when I'm finished that I realize that Beth hasn't come back out into the kitchen yet. It's a small house. Neat and clean, if cramped. There are books stacked on the floor near the kitchen table. She must study there. There's a tiny living room with a well-worn couch and a small diode TV. I haven't seen one of those in years. I didn't realize they still made them.

The hallway is narrow. I follow the light.

She's sitting on her father's bed. Her head is down. There's a photo in her hands. My heart breaks for her.

I knock on the door quietly.

She startles. Her face is flushed from crying. She puts the picture back on his dresser. "Sorry," she mumbles.

"Don't apologize for hurting."

She offers a watery smile. "I'm not used to having someone here when things go to shit."

"That really sucks." Not the most eloquent thing I could

say, but then again, I'm walking a razor's edge of my own.

I sit next to her. Wrap my arms around her shoulders and hold her because it's the only thing I can do.

It's a long time before I start talking.

Chapter Twenty-Six

Beth

He pulls out his phone. I watch him type something in and pull up a YouTube video and presses play. It's "Flake" by Jack Johnson.

"I hate this song."

I frown as he sets the phone on my dad's dresser. "Then why are you playing it?"

"I'll get to that part. Dance with me?"

I gather my dad's things and carry them into the kitchen. His request makes no sense. "I don't want to dance right now, Noah."

He stops me. The music is playing in the other room. "Trust me? There's a reason for this."

My kitchen is tiny. The table is the only thing in it that's not a cheap throwaway. I keep holding out hope that I'll stumble across an estate sale where the kids just want to get rid of Grandma and Grandpa's stuff dirt-cheap.

I look around at the tiny space. At the man asking me to dance in it. I shake my head but move into his arms anyway. He cradles one of my hands in his. His free hand presses lightly to the small of my back.

"So why are we dancing to a song you hate?"

He's guiding me around my kitchen like he's Fred Astaire. Okay, maybe not, but it's smooth and soothing.

"On my last deployment, we got bombed. A lot."

"That doesn't sound like anything good."

"It's not." He's not meeting my eyes. I'm not sure where

he's going with this, but I rest my head against his shoulder and let him guide me. I've always liked this song. "So one day, I was on my way back to my CHU from the gym, listening to my iPod."

"CHU?"

"Sorry. Containerized Housing Unit. Where I slept."

"Ah." I love the sound of his voice beneath my cheek. The deep vibration against my skin.

"I got caught in the open, and there was nowhere for me to get shelter. And the rocket attack lasted for what seemed like forever. I just laid there as the bombs went off around me. This song was stuck on repeat, and I couldn't get to it because it was in my hand."

"Why didn't you get the -- Oh."

"I got trapped beneath something. Boxes. Building. Shipping stuff. I have no idea. My shoulder was pinned down and I was trapped. I was burning, and all I could think about was turning this fucking song off."

"Noah." There is nothing I can say. No words that are sufficient. *Thank you for your service* doesn't cover things like this. Not by a long shot.

I keep dancing with him, but I no longer like this song. I've seen the scars on his shoulder, his back. The damaged tattoo shredded by raised, red scars. It didn't make sense to play this song. Not now. Hell, not ever. I would never play it again. So why was he?

"Why are you playing it now?"

"I want to change how I feel about it. I want to remember something good that happens when I hear it instead of remembering that day in the desert." He presses his cheek to the top of my head. "If I close my eyes, I want to feel your hair against my face instead of the burning sand. I want to feel your body against mine instead of the debris stabbing me. Your hand in mine instead of the iPod I couldn't turn off."

I release a shuddering breath. There is a powerful want beneath those words. It's more than a dance. More than making a new memory.

There's so much in those words. They wrap around me and crush the air from my lungs. I lift my face to his and kiss him. I kiss him until I can't breathe. Until the dance stops and my body is pressed to his with an urgency that threatens to destroy us both.

My fingers trace over the hard lines of his belly. He's pinned between my body and the counter. My tongue slides against his, the most intimate dance. I can't breathe, and I can't stop. I need this. I need him.

Noah.

I push his pants open. I want him. Now. I want to forget everything except the way he feels when he's inside me. I want to lose myself in the slide of his body into mine. I want this. I want him. Hard and fast and now.

He pushes my yoga pants down. Off one leg. Just enough that he can lift me then and then he's there, inside me. And I'm filled. Completed. He stumbles and we go down in a mass of limbs and naked flesh.

He's there, just there. He cups my face as he slides inside me once more. Slowly this time. On the kitchen floor that smells clean now, Noah fills me. The pleasure is raw and ragged and everything I need. I rise up to meet him, squeezing him with my body. Drawing out the pleasure, forgetting the pain.

For just a moment, there is just Noah and there is just me. We are the only two people in the entire world. I run my hands over his shoulders, beneath his shirt. I feel the scars beneath my touch and he doesn't pull my hands off. I urge him closer. Deeper. I want him inside me today. Tomorrow. Forever.

I look into his eyes and there are so many memories looking back at me. I'm not sure if he sees me.

"Noah." A whisper. A plea.

He focuses then. "You came home," I whisper. My fingers dig into his back as he thrusts inside me again and again. "You're home."

With me. But I can't say that out loud. It sounds like something permanent, and I am too bruised to make those promises. Instead, I arch beneath him, cupping his face.

"Say my name," I whisper. It sounds so dirty. So commanding. At that moment and always, I need to know he knows he is with me, loving him. Holding him forever close.

His eyes darken and some of the memories scatter. "Beth."

A prayer. A promise.

"Again."

He slides one hand beneath my hips, lifting me to take him deeper. "Beth."

"Again. Say my name when you come."

He shudders. My body clenches in response. I'm close. So close.

I shatter and the last thing I hear is my name on his lips as he joins me in the abyss. I am undone. Completely and truly lost.

Noah

I'm lying with her on her kitchen floor. I've been in less comfortable spots but at that moment, with Beth pressed to my side, I can't think of anywhere else I'd rather be. It's quiet now. That fucking song isn't playing anymore. Guess my phone's battery finally gave up and went to sleep. Which is fine.

I may hate that song a little bit less now. As therapy goes, I think this was fucking brilliant. Maybe I can get Beth to do it again some time when she's less fragile and I'm less broken.

I want to ask her if she'll stay with me tonight. Or if I can stay with her. She's still bruised. Still the walking wounded.

How did she do this alone?

"That was a great dance," I finally say. My voice breaks.

Maybe that's part of it. Of putting the pieces of my life back together again. Maybe I need someone else to help me do it.

She makes a warm sound against my throat. "It was a pretty great distraction, all things considered."

"Is it always like this with your dad?" I can't help it. The question sneaks out before I can stop it.

"Sometimes it's worse, sometimes not so bad." She sits up

and slips her yoga pants back on. "I think it's worse this time because he didn't have the same medication he'd been on."

"Isn't that illegal, to change someone's prescription?"

"I have no idea. I've spent so much time arguing with the bureaucratic bullshit at the VA that I have no mental space for anything remotely associated with medical law." She runs her fingers through her hair then stops, resting her head in her hand. "Thank you. For being here today."

Her words are sudden and unexpected. "Where else would I be?"

She's suddenly busy searching for one of her socks. "I don't know. Home, doing homework maybe?"

"You have a pretty high opinion of me if you think I could be doing homework knowing you're dealing with all of this alone." Her words actually hurt. I don't think she means them to, but they sting nonetheless.

"I'm just...I'm not used to having someone here." She crawls up my body to kiss me softly. "Thank you."

I hold her close because I'm terrified that one of these times, I'll let her go and it will be for the last time. I've never felt anything like this. It's powerful and it's overwhelming and it's the most potent thing I've ever experienced.

"It's what I do." A true statement. I'm used to being leaned on. I'm used to having soldiers call me, I'm used to picking them up. Beth is not one of my soldiers, not by a long shot, but for one night, it feels really good to be needed again.

If I'm honest with myself, I've missed that part of army life. Maybe it was part of what kept me functioning before I left. I have the pills. I've had the pills since the fire.

But they hadn't taken over my life when I was still in. Maybe I was just too busy to notice. It's only since I've been in school that I've been doubling up. Noticing the anxiety more. Feeling my purpose in life slipping further and further away.

I kiss her forehead. "Will you stay with me tonight?" Because I don't want to be alone. I can feel the latent panic dancing at the edge of my soul, waiting for the right moment to strike. Waiting to catch me unaware. Maybe if Beth stays, it won't be able to marshal the energy to take over my life because I'll be worrying about her rather than sitting alone with my thoughts.

I can hope. She sits up and adjusts her clothing. I do the same, not missing the fact that she hasn't answered.

"I don't know that I'm going to be fit company tonight," she says after a moment.

I place my hands on her shoulders. "I'm confident you won't be."

She smiles. "You're a pretty brave soul, aren't you?"

"I don't think you should be alone." I cup her face. "If you don't want to stay at my place, I'll stay here. If you'll have me."

She leans against me, resting her head against my chest. It's starting to become my favorite position. "I'll stay with you if that's okay?" She swipes at her cheek with the back of her hand. "I've got homework to do."

"Is your boss going to be mad that you weren't at work today?"

She hesitates a long moment. "I'm usually pretty reliable, so no, I don't think so."

"I hear a 'but' in there."

She shakes her head. "It's nothing."

I let her go. I want to push her, to figure out what she's not telling me, but she's not up for it and I don't want to start an argument.

I wash the few dishes in the sink while I wait for her to pack a bag. Her backpack is near the door already.

I pause, studying the empty pill bottles on the counter. "Do you need to report the missing pills to the police?"

She steps into the kitchen. Her hair is piled at the base of her neck. She's changed clothes. She has a small L.L. Bean tote bag over one shoulder.

"They wouldn't do anything anyway. It's not enough for them to worry about."

I frown. "How do you know what amounts they'll worry about?"

She swallows and sets her bag down, then starts shuffling

through her backpack. "We were broken into when we first moved here. They stole Dad's medication. I called the cops to report it and, well, there wasn't much they even attempted. Took a statement, gave me a police report. And that was that. I had to figure out how to get Dad meds because the doc had pretty strict rules on when they would refill a prescription."

"How did he manage?" I knew all about pain and keeping it under control. You had to stay ahead of it. Once it first started burning hot, you were fucked.

"Drinking and basically not being functional for days on end until we could get the new medication." She's avoiding my eyes now, sorting through miscellaneous papers on the counter.

"Jesus, Beth."

"It sounds worse than it is."

"No, it sounds pretty rough on all counts. How long have you been taking care of your dad like this?"

"I think my mom left when I was sixteen so...A while, I guess."

I realize in that moment that I am staring at a woman who has had to grow up a hell of a lot faster than I ever had to.

And I am awed by her.

Chapter Twenty-Seven

Beth

I'm far too used to the hospital. They let me into the back when I return with Dad's things. Noah waits outside. It's easy to see he's got issues with hospitals. I'm not surprised given his history. I'd like to ask him about it, but how do you even start that conversation? "Hey I noticed you were freaking out back in the ER. Want to talk about it over coffee?"

Those conversations don't generally go well. Like hardly ever.

I'm alone in Dad's room. One of the nurses stops in. "He's getting an MRI."

"What's the plan?" I ask. I hate that I cringe at the thought of how much an MRI is going to cost us. It's worth it. Maybe if I keep telling myself that, it will be true.

"Let me get the doc to talk to you."

I hate that non-response, but I understand that they've got their scripts they need to stick to.

I'm alone for only a few minutes - a miracle if I do say so myself - before the doctor walks in. He's young and dark-skinned with sharp features and kind eyes.

"I'm Doctor Zahid." His hand is soft and strong all at once.

He flips through my dad's chart, pausing to read whatever it is he was looking for. "You've got things pretty well lined up. Your dad gave you a medical power of attorney?"

I press my lips into a humorless smile. "That was fun trying to find a lawyer to actually prepare it. Something about a teenager making medical decisions for a grown man made a lot of them uncomfortable."

"So you've been doing this for a while then?" he asks. I don't answer and he doesn't force me to. He seems like he's got a good read on the situation. "Your dad has had a pretty rough go of it lately, hasn't he."

I smother the urge to say something smart. Alienating the doc isn't a good way to get stuff done. "That's one way of putting it," I say.

"There are a couple of things going on with him."

I brace for the list because it will be a list. A "couple" is never just two issues when you're dealing with chronic pain and everything that goes along with it.

"Well for starters, there's the back pain. Why hasn't this been treated surgically?"

I offer a tolerant grimace. It's supposed to be a smile, but I'm too worn down for that tonight. "It's a long story that involves the VA and about three years' worth of canceled appointments and surgery being classified as elective as opposed to medically necessary."

Dr. Zahid blows out a hard breath. "I've heard stories like that. I'm sorry. Your father's problems don't need to be this bad. The surgery is two-day inpatient at worst." He looks down at his chart. "Have you talked to any of our caseworkers here? There are programs designed to help fund cases like your father's."

I shake my head. My hands are sweating. "I did when we first got here, but they said that because he was a disabled vet, he had to go through the VA. They couldn't help him. Then the VA told me he was lower priority because he wasn't 100-percent disabled. And the runaround began."

"I think we can do something about that," Dr. Zahid says. "I want you to call this number and set up an appointment. Give them my name and tell them I referred you. I think they can help."

I tuck the card into my pocket. It's not the first time I've been promised help, and just like every other time, I'll follow the lead, just to make sure it's actually bullshit. Because maybe, just maybe, one of these times it won't be.

"The second thing going on is that I want your father admitted. For several reasons. First, we need to make sure whatever caused the seizure isn't a physical condition."

"That tells me you already think it isn't."

"I think it's a drug interaction. Tramadol and Flexeril are a commonly prescribed combination, but we're starting to realize that it's more dangerous than previously thought. Plus, switching him from Oxycodone to Tramadol was a risky transition to make without medical supervision. If we're going to transition him to Tramadol, then we need to make sure he comes off the Oxycodone in a controlled manner. Third, his pain is being poorly managed."

"Try not at all," I mumble.

"And we can do better," he continues, ignoring my interruption. "I want to schedule him for surgery here. In this hospital."

I look up sharply. "We can't afford that."

"You can't afford to keep using the emergency room as primary care, either."

I'm having a hard time breathing. "So that's the plan?" My lungs are tight, thinking of the medical bills. But he's right. We can't afford to keep using the ER as primary care.

"It will get him in the system and get him fixed. And his problem is fixable, Ms. Lamont. The lack of access to care is exacerbating it."

His words burn, and I want to scream at him that he's telling me things I already know. But he's trying to help. He's either offered me a lifeline or another road leading to false hope and a dead end, but it's better than standing still.

"How long will he be an inpatient?"

"A week. Maybe more while we transition him off the opiates."

"So he's really an addict."

"I think you already know the answer to that." He makes a note on my father's chart. "Your father will always be an addict.

There is no cure for this. But he's got one thing that many other addicts don't have. He's got a supportive home environment."

"You don't know that. I could be stealing his pills and selling them to my classmates for drinking money."

He is clearly not amused. He stares at me for a moment and I brace for a stern talking to but he does not justify my sarcasm with a response. It's probably just as well. "He's going to have a long recovery, even after the surgery."

"You say that like this surgery is a foregone conclusion. I don't have that much faith left in the medical system left."

He grips my shoulder then. The human connection is unexpected in the sterility of this environment. "I understand your frustration. But we've got resources to help. When your father leaves the hospital in a week or two, or however long it takes, he will have a list of appointments and his surgery will be scheduled."

It sounds too good to be true, but I'm too tired to fight, to explain that I've heard this all before. We've gotten so close to surgery that we'd went through pre-op at the VA, only to have the surgery canceled the same day. No explanation. Just *we'll try to reschedule you as soon as possible.*

"Thanks, doc."

When I'm alone, I sit there trying to absorb everything he's told me. Trying to find hope in the fact that someone, at least, believes that my dad can be fixed. That it doesn't have to be this way.

I'm not convinced. Maybe I've run out of hope. Maybe I'm just overtired.

But right now, waiting for my dad to come back to his room, there's a plan. Which is more than there was this morning.

It's all I've got. It's got to be enough.

Noah

She steps out of the hospital and my world tilts beneath my feet. Seeing her penetrates the fog in my brain like a green laser pointer aiming at the stars at night. It's like she's been discharged from the bowels of hell, a place I cannot follow her. I hate that I'm too fucking weak to stay with her while she's in there.

"So what's the verdict?"

"They're admitting him. And I have to call this woman because the doc swears there are programs to help people like my dad."

She looks defeated. "That sounds like it should be good news?" I ask cautiously.

"I've heard it all before. They'll figure out that he's not eligible for one bureaucratic reason or another."

I wrap my arm around her as we walk toward the garage where my car is parked. I don't know what to say. How do you tell someone at the bottom of the well that things will get better?

She's silent on the ride to my place and I leave her to it. Mostly because I don't know what to say. She's been through a hell of a day. Her pain is echoing off mine, stirring up memories that I'd rather forget, or at least bury beneath the pills. I'm dancing on the knife's edge and it's taking everything I've got to keep my shit together.

I carry her backpack into the house. "Go take a shower. I'll get dinner going."

She offers me a tired smile. "I'm not really that hungry. Don't cook on my account."

"You act like I'm getting ready to start a four-course meal. I was mostly thinking of grilled cheese sandwiches and tomato soup." I brush my lips against hers. "Just relax for a little while."

"I don't even know what that means." She's swaying on her feet as she shuffles toward the bedroom.

The fatigue weighing on her is practically a physical thing. She's been dealing with so much for so long by herself that I'm not sure she even realizes the ways that it's rewired her normal. She was completely functional today in a situation that would send most people into a tailspin. Civilians don't have traumatic experiences every day. They damn sure don't find their fathers face down in a pool of blood.

But she did, and she didn't fall apart. She functioned until the ambulance got there. And she is functioning still.

But the crash is coming. It always comes after the adrenaline burns off. LT taught me that the crash was inevitable, and that you needed to plan accordingly. Which is why I sent her to take a knee.

I don't hear the water running. I slide the grilled cheese off the burner and pad down the hall.

Beth is asleep. Curled on her side, her phone dangling dangerously from her fingertips. Her lips are parted, her face relaxed. The stress of the day is gone, at least until she wakes up.

I take her phone and cover her with a sheet. She can eat when she wakes up, which with any luck will be in the morning. A good eight hours of sleep will do wonders for her.

I dig through the front pouch of her backpack and pull out her phone charger and plug it in next to mine on the kitchen counter.

The silence of my kitchen is oppressive. I have homework but I can't shake the sick feeling in my guts. I've been so worried about her crash I forgot about my own.

The panic is back, twisting like bad food in my stomach. I lower my head to the kitchen table and just breathe in and out. Wishing that I didn't know how this ends.

It ends with a sleeping pill. It ends with me sinking into oblivion while Beth is here. I won't hear her if she gets up. I won't hear her if she needs me.

I will hear nothing in Princess Ambien's warm embrace, and that's exactly how she likes things. I am her slave, and there is nothing that I can do about it if I expect to keep functioning.

I step outside into the cool darkness. There's a single patio chair on the front porch, left over from the previous owners. I put my feet up on the rail and rest my head against the side of the house. The stars are brilliant points of light in the night sky.

The burning starts deep in my chest. The tightness squeezes the air from my lungs. My vision blurs and the stars are no longer bright but fuzzy. The war is circling close to the surface tonight.

"Ah fuck, LT, why can't I just let the war go?" I wish he was here to talk to. I could use some advice. I scrub my hands over my face. "I mean, I came home. I'm relatively okay. Why can't I just accept that?"

I stare up at the night sky. It's quiet. I don't actually expect a response from wherever LT is now.

"I don't know what to do." I double over, fighting the grief that threatens to break me every time I stand at the edge of this abyss.

"I wish you were here to tell me what to do. How do I unfuck this? If I stop taking the pills, I can't function. If I don't..."

I know the rational answer. Take the damn pills and stay functioning. I can't fall apart on Beth right now. Not when she's dealing with all of this shit with her father.

"I know how this story ends. We both saw it so many times."

I can't sit here alone in the dark. I go inside, grab my phone and send Josh a text. *Can you meet? Having a hell of a time tonight.*

Say where.

I leave a note for Beth in case she wakes up, but I can't stay here alone right now. I'm dancing as fast as I can on the edge of a pin, and tonight, that pin is about to stab me in the ass.

Chapter Twenty-Eight

Beth

It takes me a minute to figure out where I am when I wake up. Warm smells remind me that I fell asleep in Noah's bed. I reach out, only to find that I am alone.

There is a light on in the hallway, casting shadows in the dark. The house is quiet. I'm not used to this kind of quiet. There's always traffic around my house. The silence is actually a little unnerving because it accentuates the silence of being completely alone.

A note near my cell phone confirms my worries.

Went out with Josh. Needed to clear my head.

Part of me is disappointed that he isn't here, but I get why he left. Hell, I basically crashed on him for - I look at my phone - six hours. It's three am. Lovely. There's a tiny seed of worry, but Noah's a big boy. He's been to war. I'm sure he can handle going out in our tiny college town.

My stomach rumbles. He's got bread and a toaster. It'll hold me over. I'm not particularly fond of the idea of tearing apart his kitchen looking for something to eat. I need something other than butter, though. Hopefully, he's got some peanut butter stashed somewhere.

I open the cabinets and stop short.

Standing in a neat row like little soldiers are bottles of pills. My heart stops in my chest. I can hear nothing but the pounding of blood in my ears. It's none of my business. I'm not snooping. I just stumbled across them because he keeps them with the...peanut butter, right below them.

But *what if* is an insidious whisper on my shoulder.

My hand trembles as I reach for the first one. Oxycodone. Tramadol. Flexeril. Klonopin. Wellbutrin. Behind them, Vicodin. Percocet. A big bottle of Tylenol Three. Some with his name on the bottles. Some not.

Okay, so he's got medication.

I bite back tears because this isn't a few pain pills. Maybe on their own, each one isn't too bad, but combined, these are heavy duty. I wish I was some vapid idiot who could ignore them and not have a clue about what it means that they're here. But I know. I fucking know what these drugs do to a person.

He's been lying to me the entire time I've known him. My hand is cold over my mouth. I'm biting back a sob. My cheeks are wet and my heart, my heart is breaking in my chest. I am so goddamned tired of crying over the men in my life.

I can't stay here. I can't do this. Not tonight, after I've almost lost my dad. I can't deal with the knowledge that Noah is...I can't even think it.

I pick up my phone and call Abby.

"Hey, what's wrong?" She's clearly not asleep. Which makes me curious about why she's awake at this hour, but now isn't really the time. I'm on the edge of falling completely apart for the second time in the span of a day.

"Can you come get me? I need to get home." Abby is like me. She has a car but she doesn't drive when the bus is easier.

"Where are you?"

I love Abby just a little bit more right then. I tell her the address.

"I'll be there in ten minutes."

"Thank you."

"Do you want to tell me what's going on while I drive or when I get there?"

I cover my mouth to keep the sob restrained. "I think I better wait." My voice breaks.

But my heart is already broken. Because I am an idiot and let myself fall in love with an addict.

Again.

Noah

I didn't mean to start drinking, but the next thing I know, Josh and I have a bottle of Jack on the table between us and we're going shot for shot.

"This isn't going to end well," I say. I think I'm slurring already.

"Never does."

Josh is bigger than me. Well over six feet. He's got the tolerance of a bull moose.

He raises his glass. "Halfway down the trail to Hell..."

I raise mine in response. I know this song so well. I might have ended my career at Bragg, but I damn sure started out in the First Cavalry Division at Hood. "In a shady meadow green..."

We finish the first chorus together. "Are the Souls of all dead troopers camped, near a good old-time canteen. And this eternal resting place is known as Fiddlers' Green."

I toss back my drink, blinking hard because goddamned everything hurts tonight.

I lean forward, covering my mouth with my hand, trying to get everything locked away. The booze is hitting me hard because I doubled up on the Klonopin before I left the house.

"You ever wonder why we went?" I look over at Josh, who's busy pouring us both another shot.

"Drink. If we're drinking, bottoms ups, brother."

"How are we getting home?"

"Cab, how else? We can crash at my place later."

There's a reason I need to get home to my place, but it dances at the edge of my brain. Teasing me. I frown, staring into the glass, but I can't remember. Fuck, it'll come to me. It feels important, but the harder I chase the thought, the further away it gets.

Damn it.

"And yeah. It surprises me sometimes," Josh says.

"Huh?"

"Like I'll be listening to the radio and a song will come on from one of my deployments and I just...I go back." He grins. "There was this one time we were out in sector and my buddy Cricket was taking a piss. He looks down and he's all 'oh fuck guys'. He was standing on an IED."

"Get the fuck out."

Josh starts laughing at the memory. "No shit. He's standing there with his dick out and we're all laughing and scared shitless he's all 'you guys, this isn't funny. What the fuck do I do? I don't want to die with my dick out. Not like this anyway'."

I'm laughing because it's exactly the kind of shit that happens downrange. "Holy hell." I wipe the tears from my cheeks. I tell myself it's from laughing too hard. "So what happened?"

"We took pictures while the EOD team got him out of there."

"Oh my God, that's fucking wrong."

Josh shrugs and refills our glasses. It's going to be a rough fucking night.

"How do you turn the shit off? When you start thinking about it?"

Josh taps his fingers on the glass. He's silent for a long moment. I'm not sure exactly how long because time is kind of fuzzy at this point. Everything is numb except the hurt in my chest.

"I don't. Sometimes, I can distract myself by going for a run or something. Other times, not so much. That's when Uncle Jack comes into play."

My hands are tight on the glass. "I can't fucking be in a place like this without freaking the fuck out."

Josh pins me with a knowing look. "We've all got our demons, brother."

"Mine are winning." I roll my t-shirt up, revealing the torn remnants of my tattoo and the scars that trace over my shoulders. "I have a hell of a time sleeping without meds."

"You should talk to the doc."

"I did. They gave me more meds." I toss back my drink. "I

went in asking for help getting off the shit and they gave me more shit."

Josh pours another glass. Clearly my confession of being a goddamned pill junkie isn't groundbreaking news. "Sounds about right."

"I can't function without the shit."

"So what's the problem? You're going to one of the top schools in the country and you're doing fine. I fail to see the problem here." He pours another shot.

At this rate, I'm going to be under the table in about fifteen minutes.

I stare into the golden whiskey, his question banging around my head like a kettle drum. What is the problem? I'm fucking fine. I mean, I'm mostly okay.

I can't feel the glass in my hands. I can see my fingers rubbing the cool glass but I can't actually feel the sensation. My brain isn't registering it.

Everything is a little slow. A little fuzzy.

"I guess it's not okay if I have to spend the rest of my life doped up just to go to work every day." There's another reason. A more important one. It crashes into me, reminding me of the only good thing I have in my life.

"Holy fuck. Beth."

Josh looks at me. "The tutor?"

I drop my head onto the table, resting it on my forearms. "Fuck me."

"Dude, what happened?"

"Beth. She's been taking care of her old man since she was a kid. He's got a small problem with pills."

"Bigger or smaller than yours?"

I look up at him. He's a little out of focus. "I don't think it matters, does it? When she figures out I'm a goddamned junkie, she's going to split."

Josh shakes his head. "One, you're only a junkie if you're blowing dudes for Oxy behind a dumpster."

I laugh because that's seriously fucking wrong. "Is that the clinical definition?"

"Last I checked, yes." He pours another glass. "Look, man, sometimes the shit gets to me. I drink if I can't cope. Does that make me an alcoholic?"

"Technically, yes."

"Well, fuck 'technically.' I'm the one who needs to get my head around everything that happened downrange. I'm the one who's got to figure out how to get up every day rather than eat a fucking bullet. So fuck 'technically.' Whatever it takes to get through this shit, man. Whatever it takes. If a pill keeps you from sitting in your goddamned bedroom rocking on the floor, then so be it. And fuck these fucking fuckers for judging you for that. They haven't done what we've done. They haven't done a goddamned thing but sit in their safe little ivory towers and watch the goddamned war on fucking TV."

He ends with a shout. Several rather irritated hipsters look at us, shake their heads, and go back to their drinks.

"See?" Josh is getting wound up now. "These fucking cowards sit here and drink their fucking drinks. If we were at Bragg, we'd be fucking brawling right now. But oh no. Not these fucking pussies."

A strong hand claps me on my shoulder. "And I think that's about it, gents. Time to head out."

The bartender is one of said irritated hipsters, except that he is Josh's size with full-sleeve tattoos on both arms. "Fuck you, man," Josh says.

"No, fuck you. I paid my dues in Najaf and Sadr City. So this fucking pussy says get the fuck out of my bar."

Josh's face lights up. "No shit? What unit?"

And just like that, our night gets extended.

And all I can think about is how Beth is everything right in my world. But she's a small point of light in the darkness of the war that overshadows everything I do.

I can't forget the war. I want to. Holy fuck, I want to.

But I can't.

And I don't know how to fix what it's done to me.

Chapter Twenty-Nine

Beth

"Want to get some pancakes?" Abby asks as we pull away from Noah's.

"It's almost four in the morning."

"Which means it's the perfect time for pancakes. Especially ones with lots of whipped cream and fruit. I know a great place."

I sink down into the passenger's seat. I'm drained. Empty. I've tried to come up with a million and one excuses as to why he's got all those pills in the kitchen. But I keep circling back to the one ugly truth I can come up with.

God, it hurts to even think it.

"So what happened?" There is sympathy in Abby's voice. Not pity. I know the difference and Abby has never pitied me.

"Apparently Noah has some issues from the war."

"What kind of issues?"

I look over at her. "When did you get glasses?"

"I need them for long distances. I only wear them in class and driving. Don't change the subject."

"They're cute."

"Again with the subject," she says dryly.

"The kind of issues that need a shitload of pain pills to deal with. Among other things."

"What did you find a crack pipe or something?"

I make a sound that's mildly horrified. "No. He's just got a lot of medication."

"And?"

"And my dad is strung out on that shit. When he can't get his medication, I buy him alcohol to keep the pain at bay. He's in the hospital right now because they think he had a seizure from it. And I'm supposed to just shrug off the cabinet full of drugs Noah has?"

Abby shakes her head. "I didn't say any of that." A long silence stretches between us.

"I'm sorry," I whisper, leaning my head on her shoulder. "It's been a hell of a week."

"I know. It's okay." She turns into town. "For what it's worth, I'm sorry. For all of it. I really hoped Noah would be the real deal."

I curl my arms around my middle and slouch back into my seat. "Thanks."

"How's your dad?"

"They're doing a bunch of tests on him tonight. Admitting him. He tried to leave without being seen." My throat closes off again. "Holy hell, can this day just end?"

"Why did he want to leave without being seen?"

"Because he didn't want to pay the bills."

"Damn."

"Yeah." I glance over at her. "I think pancakes sound fantastic. Do they come with alcohol?"

"As a matter of fact, they do. Believe it or not, there's a diner that serves alcohol and amazing pancakes." She smiles. "I didn't think you were much of a drinker."

"I'm not, but you know, everyone else around me seems to be getting shitfaced on a regular basis. I'm thinking I should try it."

"It's fun on the upswing, but damn sure sucks on the downslide. Hangovers are hell on the skin."

I grin. "I'm sure you've got a cure for them."

"But of course."

She pulls up to the diner. It's in the old tobacco district. The high-end restaurants and loft apartments in the old industrial part of town.

"Who on earth comes up with the idea of pancakes and

booze?" I ask as we walk up the sidewalk.

"Someone who has clearly been in an IHOP at four a.m., but doesn't want the party to end."

There's a kitsch neon sign in the window. "Aren't there laws about when the alcohol has to stop being served?"

"Probably."

"Is this place legal?"

"I assume so," she says. "Quit worrying, will you? Let's get some breakfast. I should warn you though, that I am now obligated to hate Noah for the rest of your life because all I'm going to hear are the bad parts."

But I've stopped hearing her.

Because Noah is sitting at the bar with one of the guys from the Baywater. The bartender is leaning on the bar. Noah isn't really sitting. It's more like he's listing to one side, his head cradled in one hand.

"You've got to be kidding me," Abby says, looking between me and the men at the bar.

"What are the odds that we're going to end up in the exact spot that I don't need to be in?"

Sound fades. He's the only thing I can see. It hurts my heart just looking at him

He hasn't seen us. We can leave before there's a fight. We can turn around, and I can go home and start the long, painful process of getting over him.

I should let him explain. I should give him that chance, right? I mean that's what a better person would do. But I'm not feeling brave or good or strong at the moment. Everything inside me is breaking into a thousand pieces all over again.

It hurts so much to think about it. I can't do this again. Caring for my dad, loving him, takes everything I've got. I've been killing myself to take care of him. I don't have any room in my heart for another lost puppy.

"We should go." Abby sounds far away. Like her voice is at the other end of a long tunnel.

Noah stands up. Sways a little on his feet. Of course he does. His words are heavy and thick, jumbled together. "I'm going to hit the..."

He sees me. A thousand emotions flash across his face.

And in that instant, he knows that I know. I see the recognition, the fear.

The regret that follows quickly, draining the color from his face.

And I'm such a fucking loser that my first instinct is to go to him. Because he's been there for me this week. I wasn't alone. For once I wasn’t alone and now I am again and part of me hates him for doing this to me.

But I can't do this. I can't come home and find Noah face down on the floor. I can't manage his medication to make sure he doesn't take too much.

I can't do it.

I love him. But I can't.

Noah

It's been hours since my last shot. Josh and Eli the bartender have been swapping war stories while I've been chugging down water. I've been ready to go for hours, but I'm not going to leave Josh at the bar even if it is with his new BFF Eli the bartender who was at Najaf.

I didn't expect to see Beth at the bar. In some part of my brain that’s not completely fucked up, I realize what her being here means. It means she opened the cabinet by the fridge. It means she knows.

I don't know what to say. I stand there dumb and mute, my tongue stuck to the roof of my mouth. I try to speak but nothing comes out.

Her friend is looking at me like I'm the antichrist. Maybe I am.

"Is that her?" This from Eli the bartender.

"Yeah."

"She looks pissed."

"Thank you, Captain Obvious. That helps clarify the situation tremendously." Apparently I can talk now, so that's a plus.

I wonder if I'll be able to unfuck this before she decks me. Because realistically, I deserve it.

She has every right to be pissed.

Doesn't she? Fuck, I'm upside down over this girl.

She turns to follow her friend out of the diner.

"Beth, wait."

How original. Jesus, my inner monologue needs cue cards.

She stops. Holy shit, she actually stops. "I can't do this with you," she says, quietly. She won't look at me, won't meet my eyes.

"I've been trying to come up with a good explanation," I say. It sounds lame even to my ears.

"A good explanation for what, Noah?"

My mouth moves, but the sound is stuck again, locked in the back of my throat.

"You can't even say it." She presses her lips together into a flat line and her eyes fill once more. She looks ragged and raw from crying. "I fell for you. I fell hard. And before I fell, I thought, this is too good to be true. Turns out I was right. It is."

"It's not like that. It doesn't have to be." More hapless pathetic words have never been spoken. I'll beg if I have to. I have to explain this. I have to fix it. Everything that is right and good in my world is slipping through my fingers, leaving me alone and empty. Just like before.

"Like what, Noah? Are you going to tell me that you've got everything under control? That you don't ever take too much or run out too soon?"

Shame burns over my skin. "No. I wasn't going to tell you any of that," I whisper. "I was going to tell you I'm sorry."

That catches her off guard. She hesitates. Her mouth opens, then closes again. "Me too, Noah." She reaches up and cups my cheek in a gesture I have done a hundred times to her. Her hand is warm and soft. I want to capture her and hold her there. To beg her to let me explain. To tell her about the fire and the pain and the fucking memorial ceremonies that destroyed a part of my soul.

Instead, she whispers, "Me too."

And I have to let her go. Because I'm a lying selfish bastard, but even half-cocked I recognize the end when I see it.

There's no getting her back from this. I've broken the fragile thing that had been growing between us. I did this because I didn't tell her about the fire or the nightmares or the fear of the dark places.

I've lost her.

I've lost everything.

Again.

Chapter Thirty

Beth

"Ms. Lamont, did you hear the question?"

I look up at Professor Earl. "Sorry, could you repeat the question?"

I am acutely aware of Noah's absence in the back of the class. I can feel the empty space where he used to sit like it's a palpable thing, even with Josh still there. It's been a week, and I haven't seen him. He hasn't been in class. He hasn't set up any tutoring appointments. Not that I expected him to. I wanted to text him. To call. Just to make sure he's okay. I want to ask Josh, but every time I even think about approaching him, I chicken out because he looks so angry. Josh is Noah's Abby, I think. And I am a coward because I can't face his anger.

It's the absolute silence that worries me. And I hate myself for worrying but that's what I do. I'm the damn fool for continually picking up strays in my life.

"I asked what responsibility does the organization have to its employees? Does the business owner have an obligation beyond the exchange of a paycheck?"

I look down at my notes. I've got nothing. The last hour of class is a blur. Hell, the last week is fuzzy. I'm grasping at thin air, trying to pull something out of my ass on the spot. I pick the closest thing I can. The thing that burns on a personal level of hell. "I think organizations do have an obligation. Consider the military. They send soldiers to war, right? And when they leave the service, if they're fine, they get nothing. But what if something develops later? What do soldiers get? And what if something happened while they were in?" *What if they're burned in a fire when a building collapses on them?* But I don't say that. "What obligation does the military have to provide access to medical care if they've created problems that will require lifelong treatment?"

Parker chimes in. She's wedded to utilitarian ideals and has never considered that there is something more out there than numbers. I don't hate her most days. She's perky and blond and every jock's wet dream. She's not a complete idiot, but she's definitely here looking for her MRS degree. Which is fine, I suppose if that's the life you're from. I don't have that luxury.

"People in the military volunteered. No one held a gun to their heads and made them sign up. The military doesn't owe them a lifetime of treatment just because they may or may not have gotten hurt. How many bogus PTSD claims are out there right now? They cost the taxpayers billions because it's easy money."

I'm usually pretty even-tempered. Even when someone says something that really gets under my skin, like Parker's comment just did.

My voice is even. Barely. "They volunteer to serve so that people like you can go to college and live your life and not have to worry about things like the welfare of our country." I can't keep the emotion from bleeding into my words. "They don't volunteer to be broken for the rest of their lives because they can't get access to medical care for issues that the military caused."

"Then maybe they should have gone to college instead of joining the army," Parker says mildly. There is a smug self-assurance on her pretty features that is a serrated blade on my last nerve.

"You do realize that the military is more educated than most of the American public, right?" It's taking everything I've got to keep my temper under control. I can feel Josh watching me. I wonder why he hasn't chimed in yet. This is as much his fight as it is mine. Probably more so.

"Sure. The bottom line is that these aren't America's best

and brightest. We're talking about people who should have gone to college and didn't and now they want us to pick up the tab for the rest of their lives for their choices."

It's amazing how blasé she sounds. Not bitter. Not spiteful. Just like she's stating a fact about the weather. I suppose it's easy when it's a numbers game, which it is to someone like Parker. It's not so easy when it's about someone you love.

"I think you're forgetting that volunteers serve so that you don't have to," Josh finally interjects. "The organization that rewards its members' loyalty will find itself able to attract better applicants. The organization that thinks there is nothing more important than money will not continue to recruit the same quality of individuals."

I want to ask him about Noah. Where is he? Is he okay? But I don't.

"People are motivated by rational self-interest. You can't put a price on loyalty," Parker says.

"That's where you're wrong. Employees motivated by monetary reward are less productive, less motivated, and less trustworthy. Organizations would be smart to figure out how to optimize employees' emotional ties to their companies." Josh looks right at me, his expression filled with blame and anger, and something else. There is no mistaking that Josh is pissed. And that anger is directed fully, completely, at me. "In a functioning society, relationships are reciprocal. Exchange relationships only exist as a condition of trust. Trust is the foundation of every relationship, business or otherwise. You can't buy it."

The discussion fades, and I can't hear it anymore. All I can think about is the harsh judgment in Josh's eyes.

It takes me the rest of class to summon the courage I need. I catch him in the hall. At first I think he's not going to stop walking but then he does. He refuses to meet my gaze. "Is he...is..." I can't say the words. Fear closes of my throat.

"Ask him yourself." He starts to walk off then stops and turns back. His body radiates violent tension and I take a step back. Josh notices. "You know what? That's the fucking problem with people like you. You hear all the stuff about PTSD on the news and you rush to judge all of us as crazy fucks one bad day away from snapping."

His comment strikes a nerve, one that is really fucking tender after the last week. "You don't actually get to say *you people* to me. I've been taking care of my father - a veteran - since he came home from the war."

"Well, good for fucking you," Josh snaps. He takes another step into my space. "You get to be the fucking martyr taking care of the disabled vet. Spare me your heroics, sweetheart."

"What the hell is your problem?"

"My problem? You want to know what my problem is?" He advances toward me, stopping an inch from my face. I can feel the violence radiating off him. I try to back up again, but I'm against the wall. "You wrote Noah off. You saw the pills and you immediately decided *junkie*. You never talked to him about it. You never said 'hey, maybe this shit isn't a big deal.' You just saw the pills and looked at the shit with your dad and said 'nope, not doing this.' You're a fucking coward for running out on him. He deserves better."

"You don't actually get to judge that," I whisper.

"Yes, actually I do. I'm his friend. I've been there. Like he was for you that week with your dad. But oh no, not you. You fucking bolt at the first sign of trouble."

"He's got a goddamned cabinet full of hard drugs, Josh. What am I supposed to do? Turn a blind eye and pretend everything is fine? Until when? Until it isn't?"

"You're supposed to trust him enough to talk to him. To give him a chance to figure out what the hell is going on in his life." He looks down at me with disgust and it hurts worse than anything else. "You're supposed to stand with someone you love, not cut and run the first time things get a little rough."

He might as well have slapped me. His words stab me in the heart and rip open my chest.

I stand there bleeding from the harsh, ugly truth.

Noah

I've fallen behind in stats. Just like I suspected I would. I can barely understand what the hell regression is, let alone what residuals are and why they're important. But I'm too damn stubborn to ask Beth for help.

I saw her in class after the fight at the bar. Just once. And then I stopped going. I can see her clearly in my memory and it haunts me. She's frozen. She doesn't smile, doesn't acknowledge me. She's gone to a place where I cannot reach her. Does this hurt her as much as it's killing me? Hell, I want to fix this but I have no idea how. So I retreat. Because there's nothing else I can do.

There is an e-mail from Professor Blake after I miss my second class. *See me.* God, but those notes haven't gotten any easier since the first time I was in school. I want to ignore her but she is the one person on campus that I will not blow off. Fear is a sick knot in my belly as I knock on her door.

"Things aren't working out with the tutor?" she says by way of greeting. There are barriers between us that need to be there when we're around people. I pretend to be just another student; she pretends I'm an anonymous face in the crowd. But we both know better.

"Not exactly."

She takes off her glasses and comes around her desk and pulls me down onto the small couch in her office, the barriers gone. She's no longer Professor Blake. She's LT's mom and she's been a surrogate mom to me since I first met her years before.

There is earnest concern looking back at me and it nearly breaks me. "Talk to me, Noah. You were doing so well. What happened?"

"It's complicated." I can't bear to see the disappointment in her eyes.

"It always is." She cups my chin, forcing me to stop hiding from her.

Her smile is kind and warm. You'd never guess that she

makes the meanest scones on the planet from looking at her in Stats. She's cold and hard and demanding in public. In private, she's warm and loving and...she's the mom I wish I had. Her hand slips from my chin to rest on my shoulder. She is patient comfort and I am tempted to let myself fall completely apart. But I can't. Because I'm terrified I might not ever put the pieces back together again.

"I kind of screwed things up with Beth."

"Tell me something I don't know, Captain Obvious," she says dryly. I can practically hear LT in her voice. The same tone. The same dry sense of humor. "What happened?"

"She's been dealing with her dad's medical issues."

"His addiction issues, you mean."

"Right. Those." Shame crawls hot and prickly up my neck. The panic dances in my gut. The words are stuck somewhere between my lungs and my throat.

"You know you can talk to me, right?"

I cover my mouth, but not before the sob I've been fighting breaks free. It's been building for days. "I don't know how to fix things. I used to have a purpose. I used to know how to fix everyone's problems. And I can't even figure out how to call her and say I'm sorry. I fucked up."

"Mike always talked about you. You were the platoon's white knight. Always saving people from themselves."

"Yeah, well, what I did mattered. People trusted me. Here? Here I'm just a fucking college student who can't even do stats without someone explaining it in crayons."

"That's not true, and you're selling yourself short."

"It damn sure doesn't feel like I'm selling myself short. I'm in over my head, and I should just get out now. Go back to doing something I'm good at."

"Would you join the army again? Go back to war?" I suck in a hard breath at the harsh reality that her words slap at me. "I'm not trying to be cruel, Noah. But maybe you just haven't figured out why you're here yet."

Anger snaps past the blockage in my throat. "Don't pull the 'God has a plan' bullshit on me."

She holds up her hands. "I wasn't going to. I was going to tell you that there's a reason you're here and not back in Afghanistan or Iraq. And maybe that purpose is to be here for Beth. And me. Because knowing you're here, knowing that you meant so much to Mike means the world to me. I don't know what your purpose is, but I do believe you'll find it again." She reaches out and covers my hand with hers. The bones in her hand are fragile, her skin soft and cool. "Maybe you're here for others, just like you've always been."

Tears burn behind my eyes once more. They're hot and tumbling down my face. "Why did it have to be Mike, Sheryl? Why him?"

"I don't know." Her arm slides around my shoulders and I lean on her because I can do nothing else. "But I still have you and that has to be enough."

I cover my mouth with my hands, trying to bind the emotion back before it crushes me. "That's a pretty shitty trade-off."

"Maybe it is. Or maybe your time here on earth isn't done yet, and maybe Mike's was."

She leans her head against the top of mine, and I remember why I love her. "I will miss him every day of my life. But knowing I've still got one son in this world is enough for me."

"I'm not your son." I'm not trying to be cruel, but the words are necessary and true.

"Maybe not by blood, but you are the son of my heart. Don't try to get out of it, either. You're stuck with me."

I smile because it's the kind of thing she's always said. The first time I met her was when Mike brought me home for Christmas like a stray puppy. And Sheryl welcomed me into her home and made me feel like...like I belonged.

"I've screwed up pretty bad," I whisper.

"I'm sure it's not as bad as you think."

"It's on the level of really not good shit." I don't have the words I need. Even now, trying to confess my sins to the one person in the world who won't judge me, I'm stuck on how to say it. "I've got a small pill problem."

She doesn't move, but I feel her stiffen. "The kind of small where you're just taking a bunch every day or the kind of small where you're robbing children of their lunch money for drugs?"

I'm horrified, but I laugh anyway. "You should break this terrible sense of humor out in class. You'd be less terrifying."

"The whole goal is to be terrifying, silly boy. People won't take me seriously if I'm cracking jokes all the time." She takes both my hands in hers. "What kind of pill problem?"

And finally, I find the words.

Chapter Thirty-One

Beth

"You're not going to make shit for tips if you don't get a smile on your face. You can look like someone died after your shift," Abby says.

My phone is a solid weight in my hands and it is silent. "Noah hasn't been around for a week."

"Which is good because that means the break is clean and you're moving on. Take table five, for instance. Tall, dark and drop-dead sexy. He's been checking out your ass all night."

"Table five is yours, he's more your type, and holy cow, can you have a little sympathy?"

"No, I can't, because I'm your best friend, and my role in this scenario is to push you out of your heartbreak to a tall, dark, soothing balm like table five."

I smile and shake my head. "Don't ever change, Abs."

"I hate it when you call me that. Ab-by. 'Abs' is my least favorite body part."

"Ha."

"Seriously, take table five. Make small talk. Remind yourself that there are other men in the world."

"Says the woman who hasn't dated since she broke up with her ex?"

"My middle name is hypocrisy." She shoos me toward the table. "Now go."

I love Abby but I'm not in the mood to flirt. Still, she's given me a table and I have to make the most of it. I need the money. My call to the woman Dr. Zahid recommended has actually not ended in disaster. Except that I've got to pick up three hundred dollars in prescriptions in two days when my dad gets out of the hospital and I'm about eighty bucks short. So I kind of have to be nice to Mr. Tall, Dark Soothing Balm.

"Hi, what can I get for you?"

He looks up at me and up close, I can see that Abby isn't joking. His eyes are a dark, dark brown, the color of molten chocolate. His skin is light caramel. He's got a strong jaw and shoulders that are made for that suit. "Gin and tonic and your phone number."

I smile and try to make it genuine. "You'll have to do better than that to get my number."

There are tiny dimples in his cheeks. If my heart wasn't already bruised and broken, I might flirt with him. "Who was he?"

"Who?"

"The guy who broke your heart."

"Are you psychic or something?"

He lifts one broad shoulder. "Not exactly. You just look like you could use a good laugh. I assumed it was because of a guy."

I offer a wry smile. "Pretty good assumption."

"Any chance I can fix it?"

"What are you, my therapy godfather?" I try to take the sting out of my words. They escape before I can stop them.

He's unfazed, his eyes still warm and kind. "Nah, nothing like that. I just hate to see a pretty girl look so sad."

I roll my eyes. "We really need to find you some better pickup lines."

He laughs then and hands me his card. "Well, if you change your mind, give me a call sometime. No pressure."

"Thanks, but I'll pass. Can I take your order, though?"

The rest of my shift passes without incident or any more stray flirting. My heart hurts from the fight with Josh. I don't know how to wrap my brain around Josh's verbal slap. His was a direct hit. It cut and cut deep.

Not knowing what's going on with Noah, though. It's

killing me slowly.

I'm tempted to take the car to his house. I want to know if he's okay.

I don't know what I'll say if I see him. I just…I just need to know that he's all right.

Maybe if I keep telling myself that, it'll be true.

I shoulder my backpack and start on my walk home. Part of me holds out a little bit of hope that maybe Noah will be waiting for me outside in the dark like he used to. That he'll step out of the shadows. That he'll be okay.

The moon is out tonight, making my walk home brighter than it normally is.

His car is in front of my house when I round the corner to my street. My heart beats a little faster when I see it.

He is sitting on my front steps. His arms folded across his knees. Still. Utterly still. And waiting.

There is a rush of fresh air into the space where my heart had been. He's here. He's okay.

And then he looks up at me. And I realize that he is not okay. His eyes are bloodshot and rimmed with red. He's lost weight. He's still. Unnaturally still.

The broken gate creaks behind me as I step into my yard. Fear slows my steps as I approach. I don't know how this story ends, but I'm terrified of the different ways that it could.

"Hey." It's all I can manage.

"Hey." He swallows hard. "How's your dad?"

"He's okay."

"Is he still in the hospital?"

I nod. "Yeah. Detox didn't go so well." An understatement that stands between us, an impassable chasm.

He looks down at his hands. He scrapes one nail with his thumb. "So listen. I'm, ah, I've got to go away for a while."

"You've already been away for a week." I take another step. Because I'm an idiot, but I want to be closer to him. I want to feel his skin against mine. I want...I want him.

I don't know how to do this. So I let the silence stand when I really want to ask him where he's been. How.

"I tried stopping everything two days ago." He won't look at me. "It didn't go so well." My words from a moment ago are a slap. "I'm taking incompletes in all my classes." He finally looks up at me and there is fear and uncertainty in his dark brown eyes. "If...if I come back, will you help me pass Stats?"

"What do you mean if?" My voice breaks.

Noah

I try to swallow the dust in my throat. This is so much fucking harder than I thought it was going to be. My hands are shaking. I lock them together to keep her from seeing. "I don't know what kind of person I am anymore. I don't know who I am without the pills. There's this thing out in Colorado. It's rehab and PTSD treatment and all that."

I hadn't planned on telling her. I meant to ask her about Stats and then leave. I didn't want to worry her. I didn't want to see the pity and the disappointment in her eyes when I admitted just what the war has done to me.

I'm such a fucking liar. I needed to see her. Just once more. And the words just spilled out.

"I've been using since I was in the hospital. I've been abusing for the last year or so." The words are sticking in my throat, but I force them out. They're rough and ragged and raw. Kind of like the sand that carved its way permanently into my skin in that hot fire. "I've gotten pretty good at convincing myself that I don't really have a problem."

I finally look at her. She is bruised and battered in the moonlight, her pale skin almost glowing. "I'm not asking you to wait for me or anything like that."

"Noah." I can hear it in her voice. The leading edge of sympathy that's not quite pity yet, but it will be.

I have to finish this before I chicken out. "I just thought you should know. I'm, ah, I'm not doing this for you. I was. I was going to try. I kept trying to find the words, and life just got in the way. But..." I look down at my hands again. "If this is going to work, I've got to want it for myself. So I'm not doing it for you."

"Good." A whisper in the darkness. A surprise.

I look up at her sharply. "Well, that's hell on the ego, that's for damn sure."

She makes a horrified sound that's somewhere between a laugh and a sob. "That's not what I meant." A pause. "I'm glad you're doing this for you, Noah. Because you're right. You can't do this for me. It has to be for you."

She steps toward me then. Stops when she's close enough that I can see her pulse throbbing in her throat.

She stuns me when she drops to her knees. And leans forward until her head is resting against my shoulder, her arms sliding around my waist. She smells so good, so fucking good. I should leave. I should get the fuck out of here before I ruin this fragile truce again.

But I can't. Because Beth is in my arms again. I never thought I'd smell her hair again or feel it pressing against my damaged skin. She's my lifeline, and I never should have put her in that position.

I shudder and pull her close until she is in my lap. I can feel the wetness against my cheeks, and as long as I live, I'll never know if the tears are mine or hers.

"I miss you. Oh God, I miss you." The words tear from my throat.

"I've worried about you. I didn't want to but I did." Her arms tighten around me in response. Her words are not a promise. They're nothing.

They are everything.

Chapter Thirty-Two

Beth

My father is finally out of the hospital, but he's not ready to come home yet. The drive to the inpatient treatment center on the other side of the state is awkward and quiet. It's good, don't get me wrong. But I don't know how to deal with the reality that my life may not revolve around taking care of my dad anymore.

The phone number that Dr. Zahid had me call wasn't too good to be true. And now my dad is on his way to some holistic treatment center where he'll stay for the next month. Getting clean and getting healthy.

Without me.

I don't know how I feel about that.

"So don't burn the house down or anything while I'm gone," he says when we pull down the long gravel drive toward the address. It looks like an old plantation complete with white pillars and a drive lined with ancient pine trees.

I try to smile. "I won't."

"You don't sound very happy to be getting rid of your old man for a month."

My throat squeezes shut as I help him out of the car. "I'm scared," I finally whisper.

"Me too." He pulls me into a hug and I'm lost, holding onto my dad for dear life, terrified that I might never see him again. Which is stupid because this is the closest I've come to having him back since he first got hurt.

"I'm going to get better, sugar bear. I promise." Whispered

words I've dreamed about. "You won't have to take care of me anymore."

A sob breaks out of my throat. I don't know what that even means but I won't lay that on him. I swipe at my cheeks and try to smile up at him. "No cute nurses, okay? Because that didn't work out so well last time."

He rolls his eyes, but a flush crawls up his neck. My dad, the ladies man. Who knew? "Fine," he grumbles. "I'm going to get signed in and settled." He pauses. "You don't have to come in."

I'm not sure if I want to or not. "I'll see you in a month," he says when I say nothing.

I nod and he slips by me, heading toward the big house. I don't turn around. I can't. I wait for a long time before I slide back into the driver's seat. I can see him in the rearview mirror, standing on the porch, his green army duffle bag dangling from one hand. It's breaking my heart to leave him there but it's for the best.

I keep driving. It's the hardest thing I've ever done. But there, in the broken shards of my heart, is a single seed of hope.

***

There is a note from Professor Blake for me to see her after Stats. I'm distracted and not paying attention. Normally I'd be tense with anticipation, wondering what she needs to see me about, but there is too much on my mind.

Noah has been gone a month. I still look for him in class every day. I look for him in the shadows after work.

I haven't heard from him. I don't know if he's okay. I don't know if he's quit the program and just hasn't come home. I don't know if he's managing or if he's not and it's killing me. It keeps me awake at night when I'm supposed to be grading assignments and completing my own.

It's the not knowing that drives me slowly insane.

I knock on Professor Blake's door. There is a cream-colored envelope on her desk that she slides toward me. It's heavy in my hand. "Congratulations, Beth."

My fingers shake as I open the envelope, reading the words I'd put so much hope into. Then I read them again because they cannot possibly be real. "I start the internship at the end of the semester?"

She nods, her eyes warm and filled with pride. "You've worked very hard for this."

Words are locked in my throat. "It doesn't seem like it's possible," I whisper.

"Howard was on the fence about you. He wasn't sure a girl from your background would be a good fit." Her words should sting but they don't. They are true enough. "But Alistair was impressed by your story. He overrode Howard's objections."

I look down at the heavy card stock in my hand. "Thank you," I whisper because I am confident she had more to do with this than she's willing to admit.

My eyes blur again. I'm so tired of feeling like the other shoe is going to drop any day now. That my dad is going to be back on the couch and my normal will return to what it was. I don't know how to function without him, but I'm learning. I stayed out late with Abby after work last night. We ended up at a coffee shop talking about work and school and her distinct lack of a love life since she broke things off with Robert. I sure know how to party, right?

This internship feels like a pyrrhic victory. Something I wanted so much for so long but now it's empty and hollow. I wanted to celebrate with Noah but he's not here. But I don't say any of those things.

"He's going to be okay." Professor Blake is apparently a mind reader.

I look up sharply. "Ma'am?"

"Noah. I've known him a long time. He's like a son to me." She hands me a photo that has sat facing her computer, but away from the door. I've never seen it before.

I look down at two grinning soldiers. I recognize Noah immediately. "Who's this?"

"My son Michael."

My throat closes off as I stare down at the picture, absorbing how young and carefree and strong Noah looks.

There is sadness in her eyes. Sadness and understanding. “Noah has always been a thoughtful boy. More so than Michael. When Michael asked me to see about helping Noah out with his application to school, I had no idea how long it would be before I'd see either of them again."

Her words do something funny to my heart, knowing that she’s connected to Noah this way. "Noah said it was important that he pass all his classes."

Her smile is warm and kind. "He's determined not to screw this up. He doesn't understand how having him here is more than enough for me." Her smile turns a little bit sad. "I tell you this because I'm betting on Noah to pull through this and come out stronger on the other side. He's stronger than he knows." She pauses so long that I look back up at her. "So are you."

I swallow hard. "Thank you." I don't argue with her even though she's wrong. If I'd been stronger, I wouldn't have bailed on Noah in the first place. Guilt is an insidious thing sitting on my heart, smothering the happiness I should feel at being offered this internship.

Maybe I’m just tired. I’ll be happy about it tomorrow when I’ve had time to process it.

I head to work because there is nothing else I can do. My father is in rehab, making sure he's capable of functioning on his own before he comes home.

I am completely alone and I don’t know what that means.

I guess I’ll have to figure it out. I tell Abby about the internship and she damn near shrieks with excitement. Her happiness will have to be enough for me for now.

I'm exhausted after the end of a difficult shift. Every customer tonight seemed to be a whining diva who needed the lemon in their water at room temperature, or their asparagus had touched their bread and could they have another plate please.

I'm irritated and tired and lost in thought when I step into the darkness and head home. I want to tell my dad about the internship but I'm not allowed to contact him for another week, at least.

I want to tell Noah but I don't know how to reach him.

I am alone in the darkness, walking between the pools of light that illuminate the sidewalk. It's damp but warm on the walk, and my mace is in its customary place in my hand. I'm edgy tonight. Wary when the shadows move.

A familiar form melts out of them. A form that I recognized. A form I hadn't dared hope for.

Relief is a palpable thing that prickles over my skin. I stand there frozen for a moment. There is nothing I can do.

Then I take a step. A single, halting step.

Noah. There. Just there. So close. So very close.

And then we're both moving until he's in my arms, and I'm in his. Our mouths collide in a fierce rush of heat. My body fits to his the way it was meant to. His arms are tight around me, his skin hot and warm. His grip is fierce and strong. Like he's never going to let me go.

I am fine with that plan. His clothes are bunched in my fists. He is warm and strong and solid and real. So goddamned real.

"Oh God, I missed you."

"I missed being called God," he whispers against my mouth.

I laugh because I can't help it then lean back to look at him, really look at him. He looks rested. Whole.

He looks like Noah. Not some fractured GI put back together by pills and bad medicine. He's just Noah. My Noah.

He cups my face gently in his hands in the way that I have come to love. His mouth is warm against mine. "I missed you so much," he whispers. And then I am lost in his arms. I'm never going to let him go.

He's home.

And for the moment, it is enough.

Epilogue

Beth

I am alone when I wake up. I'm not used to it, but it's getting better. I no longer have the blazing flash of panic wondering where he is or if he's okay.

I suppose the latent worry will always be there. Trust, when broken, never goes back together just like it was. There are always fault lines and cracks, but it's up to both of us to avoid stepping on them.

It's easier some days and harder on others. I'm not sure what today will bring.

I hear the shower running. Steam rolls out of Noah's bathroom. I wonder how long he has been in there. Given that the sun isn't up yet, it's not a good sign.

I'm still navigating through this new aspect of our relationship. The one where I try not to worry and fuss over him and he works on staying sober. It's hard because I know that he is still in pain. Will probably always be in pain.

I don't know how to fix that. But I've gotten better at being there when the pain comes. It's not a perfect solution, hell it's not even a marginally good one, but it's the best we've got right now.

I slip from the bed. Sliding my pants down my hips and tugging my tank top over my head, I then pad toward the bathroom. Steam mats my hair, making it curl into my skin.

I can make out his shape in the fogged up glass of his shower door. His head is down, beneath the water. His shoulders bent.

I can hope that he's merely rinsing his hair but I'm not that naïve. Not anymore, at least. I hesitate, but only for a moment, then I open the door and step into the scalding heat with him.

His skin is hot. I slide my arms around his waist, resting my head against his back. He doesn't move for the longest moment. Water runs over my face, soaking my hair, my skin. My blood warms just from touching this man.

And from the memories of what we've done in his shower. Have I mentioned that I love his shower?

For a moment, we simply stand together, his body stiff and tense.

Then his hands cover mine near his heart. I melt a little bit more for this man. I can feel the scars beneath my cheek, the stark demarcation between smooth strong skin and the raised edges of the damaged areas. I press my lips near the edge. I want him to feel my touch. To know that I am here for him. Always. No matter what.

He turns after a moment and pulls me close. I will never get over how good it feels to be skin to skin with him. To feel his heart beneath my cheek, his arms strong around me. There is so much strength and goodness in him.

So much courage to keep on going when things are dark and difficult and others would just give up. I think he's thought about it. At night, sometimes, I find him alone in the dark, listening to "Flake", staring into the distance at something only he can see.

I sit with him on those nights because it is all that I can do. I can't take away the memories. I can't dull the pain. But I can be there for him.

He brushes his lips against my forehead, then lower until he finds my lips. I open for him, tasting the sleep and the water. I love the way he kisses me. Long, simmering kisses, slow glides of tongue and nips of teeth. He strokes the fire to life in me with the simplest touch. I burn for this man. I always will.

He cups my face and deepens the kiss. I slip my hand between our bodies, cupping him, stroking him gently. I've learned what he likes, what drives him wild. He's done the same, listening as I tell him what I like. Whispering dark and dirty things that with him are good and right and clean.

But right now, in this moment, there are no words. There is simply the slide of bodies, the caress of skin as he sinks to his knees in the shower, taking me with him. I straddle him, angling my body until he is there, just there. He stops me then.

Waits until I meet his eyes. His thumb strokes my cheek, his hands strong and familiar.

"I love you," he whispers against my mouth.

I slide down his body then, taking him deep inside me with a single motion, moving in that special way that takes us both closer to the edge of the abyss.

I dig my fingers into his shoulders, bracing myself so that I can move the way we both need. The delicious friction, the slide of his body into mine, drives us both closer to the edge of the abyss.

And then he moves and we are on the floor. The shower streams behind us but all I can feel, all I can see is Noah rising over me. His body tight and tense and driving into me. His eyes dark and haunted as he watches me. Our bodies slide together and I reach for him, pulling him down. My arms are tight around his back, my thighs gripping him tight as my orgasm dances just out of reach.

"I love you," I whisper in his ear. "I love you."

I don't know if he believes it. If he feels it deep in his soul like I do.

But I will say it every day until the end of time if that's what it takes.

Because I will never leave him alone again.

Thank You for Reading!

Thank you so much for reading! Word of mouth is incredibly important to helping authors like me reach new readers so please tell a friend if you've enjoyed this book. Reviews help other readers decide whether or not to pick up a book. If you'd consider leaving a review, I appreciate any and all of them (whether positive or negative or somewhere in between).

Want to know when my next book is available or special sales? Sign up for my newsletter at http://www.jessicascott.net/mailing-list.html

Don't miss my contemporary romance series Homefront about soldiers coming home from war.

Homefront: First Sergeant Gale Sorren & Melanie

After the War: Captain Sean Nichols & Captain Sarah Anders

Face the Fire: Captain Sal Bello & First Sergeant Holly Washington

Love New Adult? Want to know what life is like for a soldier home from war adjusting to life on campus? Check out my New Adult Falling Series:

Before I Fall: Noah & Beth

Break My Fall: Abby & Josh

If you'd like to read about my own experiences in Iraq and the transition home, please check out **To Iraq & Back: On War & Writing** and **The Long Way Home: One Mom's Journey Home From War**.

Want more stories about soldiers coming home from war and the families who love them? Check out my Coming Home series:

Because of You: Sergeant First Class Shane Garrison & Jen St. James

I'll Be Home for Christmas: A Coming Home Novella: Sergeant Vic Carponti & his wife Nicole

Anything for You: A Coming Home Short Story: Sergeant First Class Shane Garrison & Jen St. James

Back to You: Captain Trent Davila & his wife Laura

Until There Was You: Captain Evan Loehr & Captain Claire Montoya

All for You: Sergeant First Class Reza Iaconelli & Captain Emily Lindberg

It's Always Been You: Captain Ben Teague & Major Olivia Hale

All I Want For Christmas is You: A Coming Home Novella: Major Patrick McLean & Captain Samantha Egan

About the Author

Jessica Scott is a career Army officer, mother of two daughters, three cats, and three dogs, wife to a career NCO, and wrangler of all things stuffed and fluffy. She is a terrible cook and even worse housekeeper, but she's a pretty good shot with her assigned weapon and someone liked some of the stuff she wrote. Somehow, her children are pretty well-adjusted and her husband still loves her, despite burned water and a messy house.

Photo: Courtesy of Buzz Covington Photography

Find her online at http://www.jessicascott.net

Made in the USA
San Bernardino, CA
19 March 2015